To Wes [illegible]

Who saved my ass more times than I can count.

Mike Harin

Canyon

Two Dunsmuir Stories

BY

Michael Harris

Bloomington, IN

Milton Keynes, UK

AuthorHouse™
1663 Liberty Drive, Suite 200
Bloomington, IN 47403
www.authorhouse.com
Phone: 1-800-839-8640

AuthorHouse™ UK Ltd.
500 Avebury Boulevard
Central Milton Keynes, MK9 2BE
www.authorhouse.co.uk
Phone: 08001974150

First published by AuthorHouse 1/9/2007

ISBN: 978-1-4259-7758-0 (sc)
ISBN: 978-1-4259-7759-7 (hc)

Library of Congress Control Number: 2006909951

Printed in the United States of America
Bloomington, Indiana

This book is printed on acid-free paper.

In memory of:

Robert Creighton Harris, 1916-1975

Kathleen Faye Harris, 1947-2005

Grace Virginia Maddern Harris, 1917-2006

1.

Maybe John was the only one to remember it, because Annie, who sat beside him on the couch as they watched the Mallet through the window, was only four then. He was six. And even so, he couldn't remember all of it. They must have been making noise, because otherwise their father, sleeping into the afternoon after a night's work on the railroad, wouldn't have come out of the bedroom. But all he remembered was silence. This was in their old, rented house on Sacramento Avenue. The far side of the street had no houses; behind it, the land dropped off in a slope of wild blackberry bushes to the hidden tracks. The huge black cab-forward locomotive was steaming toward the turntable and the roundhouse in the center of town. It seemed to glide as smoothly and quietly as a sled against the white mountainside beyond the river, through the falling snow. The flakes had their own silent, dreamlike speed. They made him sleepy. Maybe it all *had* been a dream. But he remembered it so clearly: how when their father came out, wearing just his Jockey shorts, he looked as broad and white and cold as a snowbank, and how in the dim light of the window the shadows of the real flakes fluttered down over his chest and arms like moths, and how the folds of the sheets he'd slept on had left strange creases in his skin, like marks chiseled into rock. Their father was silent too. He took the boy and the girl both by the hair and cracked their heads together so hard their ears rang. Then he went back to bed.

# # # #

Now it was 1954, and John was ten. It was summer. They lived in a different house, on Shasta Avenue, a house they owned. But his father was sleeping again, behind an unfinished wall whose raw Sheetrock and two-by-fours gave off the smell of pitch. Maybe not sleeping, because of the pain where the boxcar had hit. But silent still. John had caught a glimpse that first night, around the side of his mother's body as she unhooked the straps of the overalls and sucked in her breath, of the great bruise over his father's butt, upper legs and back: a pool of purplish blue as dark as ink. She hadn't dared touch it. Who had ever seen a bruise like that? His father had had to lie on his stomach for two days now, yet the men from the railroad had begun calling, urging him to go back to work. His father swore – but not over the phone. Afterward, John didn't understand. Why did they call more than once, after his father had already *told* them? It hurt too much. They ought to be scared to make him mad, John thought – and couldn't they hear what was in his father's voice, the size of it, the size of the biggest bruise in the world? It was anger that pushed out through the wall and crowded the air now so that John could hardly breathe. It made no sound, but it was part of every sound he *did* hear: the dog, Cleo, scratching her ear; the click of each dish his mother and Annie stacked in the kitchen.

He went outside.

What happened later, John knows, couldn't all have happened in one day, but that's how he remembers it, will always remember it: their five or six years on Shasta Avenue poured into twelve summer hours or so, brimful, but not a drop spilling over,

# # # #

He was lying on the back porch with Cleo when the phone rang.

He heard his mother's footsteps going into the hall. Then her voice answering, though he couldn't make out her words. Then her voice, reluctant, calling his father.

So he knew it had to be the railroad again.

Silence. John found that every muscle in his body was taut as a bowstring. He heard a floorboard creak inside, as if his father had put his weight on it, getting out of bed, and then stood still in his pain before moving again. John laid his cheek down on a board of the porch, as if it were the same one. A bare pine board. It felt cool. This was the west side of the house, under the cutbank, still in mid-morning shadow.

His father moved. John listened to the steps. Three, four ... six. Then his father's voice, a rumble.

Why don't they leave him alone? he thought. *Don't they know....* But how could they? How could they know they were putting *him* in danger?

He held his breath. Another silence. Another rumble, longer. And a silence.

Then a ringing thud as his father slammed the phone down.

His mother cried out.

John flinched, even with two walls between them. He scrooched over to the edge of the porch and looked down; Cleo ducked beside him, her tags jingling. He could see the boulder wedged against the beams that held up the porch. Speckled granite, dim in the shadow and dull with mud. The spring rains had loosened it. The bank was always sliding, oozing red clay and rocks. But nothing so big before. It had smashed into the porch in the middle of the night, shaking the whole house; Cleo had howled in terror, just as she had howled once when a bear came down the mountainside and rummaged in the garbage cans. John thought of that howl now – stroking Cleo's head, listening.

His father didn't go back to bed, as John expected. His father and his mother both came into the kitchen, where he could hear them arguing.

" – you think you're *doing*?" his mother said, angrier than he had ever heard her sound.

" – a man's own wife won't support him, ain't *that* a hell of a note?"

"Don't use that kind of language with me."

Where was Annie? John wondered.

"The old man told me once, and I didn't listen. How there'd come a time when you'd have to stand without a soul to help you. Not a solitary soul. And by God – "

"Frank, call him back. Please. Right now."

Maybe she wasn't angry, John thought. Maybe she was scared. And that was even worse; that was even harder to believe.

"What's it take to make you understand?" he father said, and his voice seemed to take on the dark and ugly color of the bruise. "You think life is all pretty grammar and church socials? You think that's how the SP runs? They ran the whole state of California for forty years, you know that? This is *it,* Connie. If I knuckle under now, I'll never ... they'll *have* me. Don't you see? They'll have me right – "

John buried his face in Cleo's warm side.

"Call him back. Please."

"Even my own wife. I thought I'd never see the day."

The thing was, John's mother had never been scared. She had always acted as if there was nothing to be scared *of.* This didn't keep John and Annie from tiptoeing around the house when their father was in a bad mood -- but in another way it helped. There was a promise in her calm, bright voice. When they grew up, they felt, they had a chance to be like her. Unafraid, even sitting at the same table with him.

But not now.

Cleo's dusty brown hair tickled his nose. Suddenly he was about to sneeze – and was twice as frightened: They'd know he was there.

A coward. A sneak.

" – think of the *children,*" his mother was saying, "if you can't – "

But then Annie's voice chirped up; she had come from somewhere else in the house. John heard her abruptly go quiet, as if she realized what was happening. But when his mother and father started talking again, their voices were normal. They weren't arguing anymore, not in front of her.

Holding in the sneeze, he slipped off the porch and ran.

# # # #

John was stunned. He was used to the silences, but he had never heard his parents argue this way before. Almost fight. He wondered what it meant, what it meant for *him* ... but he almost forgot about it when he left the house.

That summer he was two boys. One was the coward and sneak he felt he was becoming. But the other was still an ordinary kid. He became that kid now, and he might have remained that kid all day if his father hadn't been hurt – had been called out on a trip on the railroad. It all depended on Frank Hiller's pickup truck. A big maroon Chevy. Nobody knew for sure when a trip would end. If John came home and the truck was there – he remembered this half a lifetime later – he would change, inside his Keds and T-shirt and jeans, right where he stood on the street.

2.

The ordinary kid had a gun.

Gary Grissom was telling him, "You've gotta be a Jap."

"I don't want to be a Jap," John said.

"Somebody's gotta be," Gary said. "You and Freddie be Japs."

He looked at Freddie Ordoñez. Freddie didn't want to be a Jap either, he could tell. But Freddie was two years younger than John and Gary, a year younger than Gary's brother, Jimmy. So he had no choice. Besides, Freddie was half Mexican, so he looked more like a Jap. Whatever a Jap looked like.

"*Somebody's* gotta be a Jap," Gary said.

John hesitated.

They were huddled under the front steps of the Grissoms' house. It was cool and shady there. The masses of leaves on the oak trees swayed outside, and sunlight flickered through the cracks in the boards. Flecks of white paint stuck to Gary's bare back. It was tan, the way John's back never got. Tan and smooth and hard. And Gary's elbows were pebbly and rough, as if he'd rubbed them on sandpaper. John had tried to rub his own elbows, once or twice, but they just got red and sore; the skin didn't change. It wasn't fair, he thought. How just the kind of skin Gary had seemed to give him the right to decide who had to be a Jap. And all of them knew it.

"Then you be a Jap next time," John said.

Gary thought about that. "OK," he said finally. He took out his pocket knife and flicked it; it stuck in the dirt. He looked up, squinting. "Then you guys get on out of here. We gotta plan some strategy."

"Let's be Germans," Freddie Ordoñez said. "I don't want to be a Jap either."

"Japs or Germans, what's the difference?" John asked.

But he knew, or thought he did. Nobody could say Freddie looked like a German.

"The Germans were tougher," Freddie said.

Gary wouldn't give in. "The Japs were tough too," he said. He picked up his knife and wiped the blade on the legs of his jeans. "C'mon, I'm tired of fightin' Germans. You be Japs this time."

Then Mr. Grissom called from the porch. His sons leaned their heads out.

"Jimmy. You do what I told you?"

"Yes, Pa,." Jimmy said.

"You get them toys picked up out back?"

Mr. Grissom talked different. It was a twang, John's mother had told him. An Oklahoma twang. The Grissoms were Okies. A lot of Okies had come to California during the Depression, when she was a girl. "They had a hard time," she said. Still, John got the feeling that she didn't think they were quite as good as the Hillers. The Grissoms were new in Dunsmuir, for one thing. Mr. Grissom worked at the Commercial Garage downtown. He wore jeans and a faded blue work shirt, and as he clumped down the steps he carried a heavy toolbox that made the muscles in his arm stand out like ropes. He was strong, like John's father. But where Frank Hiller was solid and fair, Mr. Grissom was lean and dark and stringy, as if the sun had baked everything else out of him. His pale eyes squinted, just like Gary's.

"Yes, Pa," Jimmy said.

"You help your ma when she asks. She's got cleanin' to do.... Gary, you hear? We got church tonight." He stared at Jimmy. "You *sure* you picked up them toys?"

"I ... I will, Pa. Just a minute."

"You'd better," Mr. Grissom said. "If I find out any different, you'll wish I hadn't."

He hitched up the toolbox, so that muscles moved all down his back, under the shirt. He tossed it one-handed into the trunk of his car, a dusty black '49 Ford, and drove off slowly, bumping over the tree roots in the yard. Jimmy watched him, open-mouthed. *He's scared too,* John thought. Maybe he ought to be nicer to Jimmy from now on ... though usually he thought Jimmy wasn't very smart. But Gary didn't even blink. He just folded his knife and put it back in his pocket. John wished he could be that brave. Then he thought: *Maybe his skin's so tough it doesn't even hurt when he gets whipped.*

"You go to church on Wednesdays?" he asked.

"Yeah, ever since we joined up here. Sundays, too.... We're Southern Baptists." Gary gave him a quick look, almost shy. "You want to come?"

"I don't want to miss the Lone Ranger." It was on the radio at seven.

John grinned, then wished he hadn't.

"I mean it. C'mon. I'll ask my folks.... It'd be OK."

"I don't know."

"Are you saved?" Gary asked. Now he wouldn't give up on this either.

"I don't know.... I guess so."

John didn't want to make Gary mad, but nobody had ever talked to him this way before. Maybe the Jehovah's Witnesses who came to the door sometimes, but not just another kid.

"No guessin' about it." Gary shook his head. "You're either saved or you ain't. And if you ain't, you're goin' to Hell, sure as shootin'."

"Maybe I'd better ask *my* folks."

"Tell 'em," Gary said. "Tell 'em those other churches might be the churches of God, but this is the church of Jesus Christ."

He looked so serious, squatting under the steps in his naked skin, repeating words some grownup – a preacher? – must have told him. John felt embarrassed – for himself or for Gary, he wasn't sure. He tried to imagine himself asking somebody if he was saved. He couldn't. But Gary was brave. That was why he could tell them what to do. It must be hard, being brave like that. Awful hard.... Suddenly John was sorry that he'd tried to argue.

And he thought of something else, remembering the muscles in Mr. Grissom's back as he'd tossed that toolbox into the car so easily: Who would win, if Mr. Grissom and John's father had a fight? It was strange. He'd never asked himself that question before – never had any doubt.

"OK, we'll be Japs," he said. "Just give us a head start. OK? Ten minutes."

# # # #

He remembered a time at a Cub Scout den meeting when *he'd* told people what to do and they'd done it, like magic. They'd gone to a jamboree down in Redding and seen stuff other Cubs had made: wood carvings, baskets, rope knotted and lacquered and pinned to boards. One pack had made suits of armor out of cardboard, like knights had worn in King Arthur's time. John got so excited that he spoke up, for once. It all came jerking and tumbling out of him, how they ought to do it too. And they listened! That was the amazing thing. He expected them to laugh, but they didn't. Mrs. Garamendi, the den mother, smiled at him under her thick glasses, surprised.... But that was the trouble. Why did Mrs. Garamendi have to be surprised? And why did John feel he was standing off to one side and watching himself, waiting for the laughter? Why did it seem like magic? Not real. He didn't think Gary ever felt like that. But John had tried to act as if it *was* real; he'd gone home and made his own suit of armor, begging cardboard boxes from the S&J Market, cutting out pieces and tying the joints with string, painting them silver. He'd made a fiberboard shield, painted yellow, with a black dragon on it and the words DEATH IS BETTER THAN

DISHONOR. He'd made a wooden sword with an aluminum pie plate for a guard, punched with holes in intricate patterns. His mother had given him a pink-and-purple ostrich plume from her cedar chest to stick on the helmet. All he needed was a horse, and someone to joust with.... And then, at the next den meeting, he discovered that nobody else had done anything. He wasn't surprised. (That was the trouble again: that he wasn't surprised.) He supposed he ought to get mad, try to shame them, get them excited again.... But his own excitement was gone, and so was the magic. Nobody cared as much about armor as he did. That was the truth. They might have thought they did, for half an hour, but they didn't. Now they just wanted to be left alone, the way he usually did. He understood that. It was too much work to pull them all, like a locomotive pulling a string of boxcars, with just his idea. Too hard....

He felt a terrible weakness, the way he felt when his father was angry at him. How could Gary fight it? he wondered. And he thought: *Well, if Gary wants to run a war, the least I can do is help him.*

# # # #

By now he and Freddie were running through the Grissoms' back yard: wash flapping on the line, gnarled apple trees, tall grass with green-and-yellow foxtails. They stooped, still running, and threw them at each other, but Freddie had his shirt off too: nowhere for the foxtails to stick. Then they reached the woods.

"Do I *gotta* be a Jap?" Freddie asked.

"It's just pretend," John said. "Don't worry."

"I want to be a German."

They were scrambling uphill, a rocky path of red clay. Something stubborn and whiny in Freddie's voice made John pause behind a big fir tree. "We gotta keep moving," he panted. "They'll catch up with us." And then, when Freddie shook his head: "Well, why don't you *be* a German? You don't have to tell 'em. Just let 'em think you're a Jap. It's OK with me."

3.

A joke.

That's what they all thought it was. Just because he got hit in the ass.

Even by a boxcar.

They couldn't help it, Frank Hiller thought during those days on his stomach, unable to sleep at night, only half awake the rest of the time, sweaty and feverish. It was human nature. Still, it pissed him off. He could eat only a little of the food Connie set on the floor beside his bed. Cleo ate most of it. She leaned her chin on the mattress and nudged him with her cold nose, curious. The kids peeked in through the door but came no closer. Once or twice, he staggered to the bathroom and squatted above the toilet without any skin touching the seat and still nearly passed out from the pain of bending his back and legs. The urine that dribbled into the bowl was bloody. Connie offered to bring something from the kitchen to use as a bedpan, but what good would that do? In bed or out, he'd have to move, raise some part of himself. Why couldn't she figure that out? Sometimes the woman had no sense. Though she *cared*, at least. Give her that much. His conductor, Will Jamison, had tried to sound sympathetic on the phone but couldn't keep a chuckle from creeping into his voice. *Hit in the ass. Damn.* He could imagine Jamison fighting a grin on the other end of the line. *It can't be all that bad, can it, boy? Got plenty of padding back there.*

"Doc Reed check you out? Nothing broken?"

"No." *Except for every last blood vessel I've got back there.* "He just said bed rest, give it time."

"Well, far be it from me to argue with Doc Reed. But still. How much time does he think you'll need? Just a ballpark figure, now."

"As long as it takes, he said."

"Well, that's fine, for him. Doc Reed ain't in the business of moving trains. But we can't have you making a vacation out of it, can we?"

A vacation? Frank Hiller thought. It puzzled him at first, what Jamison was getting at. No skin off *his* nose if he had to find another brakeman. It was Frank himself who lost money if he had to lay off. The way the Southern Pacific worked, a young brakeman was stuck on the Extra Board until he built up seniority. Anybody with more seniority could bump him off a job. A young guy got bumped all the time. He had to fill in, take the scraps nobody else wanted. Work was scarce enough so that he never laid off voluntarily if he could help it. Only now, with fifteen years in, was Frank able to work steadily with the same crew for weeks at a time. He was just getting to know Jamison – a man who looked as weather-beaten as a cowboy but who kept a chess set in the caboose and insisted that all his brakemen learn to play; a Mason who studied secret ritual from a little leather-bound book in his bib pocket. One of the old-school conductors, from the days when trains had no radios and a crew had to deal with everything from hotboxes to avalanches by itself. The old guys were masters, some of them. During the Depression, even a very smart man might never have a chance to go to college. He'd end up in overalls instead, with a sun-blistered neck and grease under his fingernails. Like Frank himself. The quality was falling off, Jamison complained. These days, a kid with any brains at all *went* to college and stayed off the railroad. Frank nodded. He liked to think Jamison saw him as an exception. But what was this phone call about?

A vacation? *Let it happen to you and see what you call it.*

But Jamison surely had been hurt himself, more than once. He knew how it was. He had helped Fred Ordoñez ease Frank into Fred's car for the ride to the doctor's office. Frank had to kneel on the passenger seat and face the rear so that none of the bruise touched the cushion. Jamison said, "Good luck, son. Hope it ain't as bad as it looks," and seemed to mean it – then. This joke business -- the hint of a chuckle -- came later. Now it was as if Jamison was trying to tell Frank more than he was saying.

But what?

"Level with me, Will," Frank said the second time the conductor called. "You know I wouldn't stay out if I didn't have to." At least he hoped Jamison knew this – but then, how could he, on such short acquaintance? "Somebody thinks I'm dogging it, goddamnit, have 'em come over here and look."

Look at what? he imagined Jamison thinking. *Your purple hind end?*

"That ain't necessary, Frank. Nobody questions you've been hurt. It's all in the incident report. I signed it. But there's some ... well, just at this particular time, folks in high places, they see it as a *marginal* injury – that's the word they'd use, nothing broken and all. Not like the thing hit you in the *head,* right? Though if you ask me, you'd have been better off if it had. Gave as good as you got. A hardhead like you." Frank heard the chuckle now, but it wasn't as convincing as the silent one. Nor did Jamison usually chatter on like this. Frank was so furious at the word *marginal* that he didn't realize until after he hung up how embarrassed the man must have been. Passing on a message Jamison didn't agree with but had been ordered to give: "The safety picnic's coming up."

"That's it?" Frank asked.

"That's it."

The SP safety picnic was an annual event. Long tables of potluck at the Mount Shasta City park. Tubs of beer. Softball games. Railroad caps and buttons for the kids. Bigwigs from Shasta Division headquarters and even from San Francisco would brag about the company's near-spotless safety record: so few man-hours lost to injury in the average year that it was hardly worth the piddling effort to count them.

The safety record wasn't a lie, exactly, Frank thought, but nobody took it seriously, either. Maybe the government did, but not the men themselves, not the Brotherhood. If the SP wanted certain numbers, he had always thought, it would get them. So it was hard to imagine the company having to muscle *him,* now. Was this year worse than usual? He had no idea. Was the Shasta Division so close to some bad number that his bruised backside, if they counted it – and they'd have to count it if he laid off – was enough to push them over the line?

Maybe.

But then he thought: *This is crazy. I'm too small a fish for them to worry about. Connie's right. My temper's getting the better of me again. I must have misunderstood Will, that's all.*

It was the fever, Frank thought -- the wooziness that came over him from the heat; from staring for hours on end at the pattern of bright new nailheads in the studs by the head of the bed, raw pine smelling of resin; from listening to kids playing outside, cars passing, the burp of somebody's chain saw, the grinding of the bulldozers on the freeway cut that was going to bury this house and all his work on it. No wonder the owners had sold it to him so cheap. Four thousand dollars. They'd probably already known about this Interstate 5 project and laughed at him all the way to the bank. The state would pay him, of course – the same four thousand. Market value. But it wouldn't pay a dime for all the hours he'd put in, all the hope and sweat.

Frank Hiller, who had learned what the exact freeway route was going to be only when the grading began, felt outraged all over again. It did a man no good staying indoors like this, he thought. Lying there helpless. Nursing grudges. The bruise felt as thick and stiff as a board, yet it burned at Connie's lightest touch, so now she just poured lotion out of the bottle. Lately he'd had the sensation that his body was trying to absorb the thing, suck all that dead, clotted blood back into itself. *That* was crazy.

Wasn't it?

But when Jamison called the third time, Frank could no longer ignore the truth. The SP really was trying to force him. He had thought he could work on Jamison's embarrassment – saying, *It isn't right, Will.*

You know that. Why don't they know that? -- but it came to him now that Jamison wouldn't have *been* embarrassed if the pressure from above hadn't been too strong to fight.

"Time's running out, son." The chuckle was gone. Somebody must have taken Jamison to the woodshed, Frank thought – told him to stop screwing around and get the message across or else. "We've been lucky so far. Schedule gave us a little slack. But any time now we've got to saddle up again. And you'd better be with us."

"Will – "

"I ain't got all day to jaw with you, Frank. You got a family, don't you? Sure, you do. Nothing much you *can* do but suck it up. Better get used to the idea."

Frank clenched the phone, felt his pulse hammer at his temples.

"What about the Brotherhood?" he asked finally. That was the Brotherhood of Railroad Trainmen, their union.

"The Brotherhood," Jamison said, "has got to pick its fights, son. And this ain't one of them."

Not when it's only your ass.

# # # #

The pain wasn't even the worst of it, Frank thought. The shock of being hit was. They'd been bringing a freight down from Klamath Falls, on the North End Pool, and at Cantara Loop, the steep grade just north of Dunsmuir – the line doubled back on itself like a paper clip; he could see the caboose going in the opposite direction right above where he, in the middle of the train, was checking the brake hoses and couplings between cars – they jumped the tracks. Four boxcars, two flatcars, a tanker. It wasn't too bad, as derailments went. No cars actually tipped over and fell into the river. Thank God they were moving so slowly then. But it wouldn't have happened at all if the goddamn SP had kept up the track and roadbed properly. They'd rather save a buck or two in the short run, and what happened? Men got hurt.

Afterward, Frank remembered the banging and jolting and screeching, the red cutbank flashing by, cinders pulverized by the bouncing steel wheels, men yelling. But only afterward. The rear end of the boxcar behind him jackknifed out to the right and the swinging front end slammed into him. At a slightly different angle, he thought later, it would have crushed him against the flatcar ahead. It would have knocked him off the train, for sure, if he hadn't caught the ladder beside him and held on by instinct. Instinct was all he had going for him at that moment. Because the *weight* of the thing ... how could he explain that to anybody? Connie? Jamison? *Dead weight.* Those words meant something to him now. Tons of steel, tons of whatever that boxcar was loaded with ... all had tried to squash him like a bug. Less than that. Like nothing. The shock of being nothing, nothing at all, against so much force had driven every other feeling out of him. It had run right through him and shaken apart something inside – his bones, his atoms – that might never come together again. Even now, in the stifling bedroom, he felt a chill thinking about it. About how the world could kill you and not even blink.

Damn it, that's no joke.

But he knew they couldn't help thinking it was, all the same.

# # # #

This morning he felt a little better, finally. He had an appetite for Connie's eggs and biscuits. He scratched behind Cleo's ears when she came to visit. He heard Johnny go out, heard little Tommy laughing with the womenfolk in the kitchen. He actually slept for a while and woke up at 9:51 by his railroad watch. He could feel the warm peace of the morning filtering through the walls, broken only by the barking of Thelma Hoffman's dogs next door. What was eating *them*?

Just another couple of days, he thought – if I lay off for just one trip – I'll be OK, maybe. He gingerly pushed up from the bed, and it didn't seem to hurt quite as much. He tried to look around himself, over his shoulder. The bruise, from what little he could see of it, had become spotty. More blue than purple, with a tinge of yellow around the edges of it. As if he *was* absorbing it, somehow, after all. Swallowing his own blood.

But when he put his feet on the floor and stood up to go to the bathroom, the pain clamped him as hard as ever.

Damn.

A couple more days at least, he thought, no matter what the bastards say.

Then the phone rang, and this time it wasn't Jamison but the division Trainmaster himself.

4.

Why is he so *angry*? Connie Hiller had begun wondering again. That's what she could never understand. Her father hadn't been like that. A wide, calm man who never raised his voice, never laid a hand on his girls. He had no need to. They had only to sense that he was disappointed in them somehow. Then his voice got sad. That was more than enough. Her father had what Frank jokingly called a "great stone face" – a *graven* face, she thought to herself, as if it belonged on a dollar bill. He had lost most of his hair in a flu epidemic in Oakland in 1925, when her mother had died. Connie had been five then. She had only a vague, warm memory of her mother – a sleeve with lace on it, a caressing hand. A face shadowed by dark hair. But her father had taken care of them. He had remarried and, Connie remembered, never failed to praise her stepmother after every meal, even if the roast had been burned or the vegetables boiled into mush. "That was just lovely, Nellie," he would say. He had worked as a plumber and then as an industrial arts teacher at Tech High, and had never been out of work, even during the Depression. He had sent both his girls to the University of California (and would have sent their half-brother, George, too, if he hadn't caught encephalitis at eighteen). They rode the streetcar to Berkeley and both got their teaching credentials. Her sister, Henrietta, had taken a job at a school in Tupman, in the oil patch outside Bakersfield, and married a Navy man, even taller than Frank, from a big family of roughnecks. Connie had gone to Dunsmuir and married a railroader. Neither man had a college degree. Had the Weldon girls married b*eneath* themselves, as some of their relatives hinted? It hadn't seemed that way. Frank and Wylie both were vital, ambitious young men; they blew into the girls' lives like a gale of fresh air. Frank was a reader, too. He had made her laugh, made her feel as safe as her father had....

But why so *angry*?

This thing about the Southern Pacific, now. They shouldn't be badgering him to go to work – she was as indignant about that as he was – but he took it personally, in a way she couldn't. He *hated* the railroad, when it was just a company, out to make money..What else could you expect of it? When he hung up on the Trainmaster, it frightened her. She had stopped teaching to have a family. If Frank lost *his* job, how could they...?

"What do you think you're *doing*?" she cried.

Then they had the argument.

# # # #

Frank didn't go back to rest, though she urged him to. He shuffled into their bedroom but stood beside the bed instead of getting in. He looked out the window, through the thin lace curtain. It bothered Connie – could somebody see him from the street, naked except for his Jockey shorts? She wanted to say something, but didn't. Frank just stood there. The back of his neck and his lower arms were tanned; the rest of him was white, except for the bruise. He held his head at an odd angle. The set of his face, turned away from her, was forbidding – and irritating, too. She waited a minute longer for him to speak – to apologize? – and went out.

It did no good, Connie had decided, to wish for one of Frank's moods to end before he was ready. But ever since his disappointment over the freeway burying their lot, the angry silences had grown longer.

Last month she had decided to take them all for a picnic at Soda Creek, south of town, and Frank had almost refused to go. Maybe it would have been better if he had. Because he'd sat out in the car by himself, listening to a ball game on the radio, while the kids looked nervously back at him out of the corners of their eyes and she struggled with lighting the fire, roasting the hot dogs and marshmallows on sticks. All the fun had gone out of it. "Why are you acting like this?" she'd whispered, bringing him a paper plate of food, and he'd muttered something scornful about *togetherness*.

As if it was a stupid word for a stupid fashion – something that, by God, he wouldn't even pretend to follow.

But what was wrong with togetherness anyway? Weren't they a family?

So, fine, Connie thought now. *Just sulk.* Even though the sight of the bruise still made her wince, and she was still frightened. *But call him back, Frank, please, before he gets too upset.*

She decided to vacuum the living-room rug; the noise would drown out even her own thoughts. Tommy, who was four, played with blocks in a corner. Annie – still at the age when housework seemed a game – came behind her with a toy carpet sweeper. Annie wore a cowboy hat and a long-sleeved, red-checked shirt. She had freckles like her mother, and dimples. She made vacuuming noises: "Rum, rum!"

At least fifteen minutes went by. Then Connie turned off the machine, and that's when she heard him moving.

"Where are you going?" she said in alarm.

Frank was dressing himself. He had dragged on a pair of old brown slacks and a sport shirt, doubled over, huffing with pain; she sucked in her breath once again as he pulled the cloth over the bruise and buckled his belt. Then walked slowly into the living room. Against the light from the front window he stood, still bent, with his hands on his knees, glaring at her.

"Daddy, where are you going?" Annie echoed.

She clung to her mother's leg; Connie had to steer her along, gently, as she followed Frank.

"What do *you* care?" he muttered – not to Annie but to her.

"You should be in bed," Connie said. "If you aren't well enough to work, you shouldn't be going out anywhere."

"Ross thinks I should work." Ross was the Trainmaster.

"Call him back. I told you – " But Frank had turned away; he was walking again, toward the door. She could see the muscles moving in his back as if they were lines of pain radiating upward. "I'll call him myself. Please – "

But she was always conscious of Annie beside her, and she couldn't raise her voice.

"You going fishing, Daddy?" Annie asked.

Frank made a noise she couldn't describe – less a laugh than a bark. "Something like that, honey. More like hunting, maybe." He was out on the front porch now, still moving away. The boards creaked under him. "Hunting for another family, maybe. Somebody who gives a good goddamn."

"Frank!"

But even now she couldn't scream, even against the noise of the bulldozers off on the freeway cut to the north, and those dogs next door. She felt exposed out on the porch, where all the neighbors could see. Yelling like some trashy woman – Mrs. Sykes, maybe. Making a spectacle of herself. In front of Annie, too. But she *wanted* to scream. She had always told herself that she would leave any man who hit her – secure in the knowledge that no decent man, like her father or Frank, would ever hit a woman. But this was *like* being hit. Saying such a cruel thing in front of an eight-year-old! She felt numbness spreading over her face, as if from the blow of a fist. He limped down the steps without looking back – except once, struggling into the cab of the pickup, when he raised his eyes at her, just a second. Still glaring. Then he slammed the door so hard that the truck rocked.

And drove off.

# # # #

She couldn't call the Trainmaster – a man she hardly knew. It might make things worse. Unable to think of what else to do, she walked

Annie back in to the kitchen and peeled her a banana, sliced it up and let her eat it in a bowl of milk and sugar. "Maybe he *is* going fishing," she said. "Maybe he'll bring us some nice trout."

"Where's his rod, then?" Annie asked. "And his creel?"

She sighed. "Maybe he'll come back for them." The girl was too sharp to fool for long. "Maybe he's just gone down to the crew dispatcher. To see how long till they call him." Connie still felt numb. She braced her hands on the drainboard and closed her eyes and tried to remember her first year in Dunsmuir, 1942, when she was a brand-new teacher at the high school, "batching" with two other young women in Mrs. Polonski's basement on Sacramento Avenue, next door to the house she and Frank would eventually rent. The town was full of excitement then. The war was on. Troop trains came through, and trains with tanks and artillery on flatcars. The Army posted guards at the tunnels to prevent sabotage – this was the main north-south rail route for the whole West Coast. On weekends Connie helped the Red Cross down at the depot, serving coffee and doughnuts to the soldiers. That was how she met Frank. She would never tell him – never in the world! – but he first struck her as a homely man. He had a big nose and his ears stuck out; he rolled side to side when he walked, his arms swinging across his body. When he first asked her out, she was cool. That had been enough to discourage the few boys who had approached her in college. *Very* few. But it didn't discourage Frank. Not at all. He kept on asking, and joking with her, and Connie discovered that behind that first line of her defenses there was nothing.

Before she knew it, she'd let him take her to a baseball game. Frank played first base for the Dunsmuir Railroaders. His uniform was white flannel, a blue D over hie left breast. He had his own big mitt and spiked shoes made of kangaroo leather. He let her touch them, feel how light that leather was, like the webbing of a bat's wings. He drove her to the ballpark in what would become the first of their Chevrolets, a tan '41 coupe, and never stopped talking – never gave her a chance to get nervous. He bought her a hot dog and an orange soda and led her up into the grandstand, its wooden seats soft and splintery with age. He pointed out the clay bank in left and center field, with the fence at the top of it and trees beyond that. Only one man had ever hit a ball out of the park in dead center, he told her – and that was Babe Ruth himself.

"Babe Ruth!" Connie said, smiling and shaking her head. The soda fizzed in her nose. This had to be another joke. "What could he have been doing here?"

"Barnstorming," Frank said. "He came out here in '24, him and Bob Meusel of the Yankees, and played an exhibition game. I've seen pictures of it. Ths old park looked just the same."

Somehow this made her laugh – she wasn't sure why. "Such a historic place. I'm honored," she said. Could this be her? Joking back? The grandstand offered shade, but she couldn't see him as well as she wanted through the screen that caught foul balls. Around the third inning she ventured out to the open bleachers behind first base, with the street at her back. She wouldn't remember what Frank did at bat. Maybe he was trying too hard. What she did remember was him standing crouched beside the base, yelling at the hitters on the other side, yelling at his own pitcher: *Hey baby, hey baby, just burn it in there, he's got nothin', got nothin', babe, just a girl up there, hum babe, hum babe!* Connie was amazed at this. She had grown up in a house full of women (except for George, who was so much younger). Her father had little interest in sports. She had never seen a baseball game before – not a game played by grown men with sunburned necks and stubble on their chins. They insulted one another terribly. One man on the other team chewed and spat tobacco. They yelled on the field, and they yelled in the dugout when it was their team's turn to bat. *Old lady up there, old lady, gotta roll the ball up there, he can't throw it, hey baby, got nothin' up there, you can hit him, got nothin' at all.* Connie had feared such loudness and crudeness all her life, but today she found it exhilarating. They were *boys*, she thought. Just boys, and having a wonderful time! She watched the Dunsmuir shortstop, Behnke – "that big dumb Dutchman," Frank had called him – with a gaze that seemed purified by the smell of grass, the cheers of the crowd and the slant of the sun over the western mountain, full in her face. Behnke, Frank had given her to understand, had a scattershot arm; he would throw at Frank's feet or a mile over his head – everywhere but where he was supposed to. This was true, she saw, though Behnke could hit. Twice he sent great cracking drives to thud into the bank in left field, lumbering into second as the outfielder scrambled for them up the steep red clay. And she saw, with the same sudden clarity, that Frank almost *wanted* Behnke to throw wild, just so he could rib him about it later. It was a kind of strange love that these men had. It shimmered around her in the Sunday afternoon light and warmed her like the sun, which already had begun to give her face and upper arms a painful blush. The very last enemy batter – for they were *her* enemies now – grounded hard into the hole between third and short, and Behnke lunged, caught the ball and threw off-balance into the dirt, and Frank dug it out neatly and stepped on the bag. It was a perfect ending. And then he *sauntered* – there was no other word for it – with the whole grandstand watching, over to where she sat, as if carrying a bunch of long-stemmed roses, and handed her the ball, scuffed by the dirt, with a round grass stain on it like a kiss.

# # # #

It had seemed like an adventure at first, buying this house, Connie thought – in this quaint little town, in this beautiful country. It was a fixer-upper, of course, but *theirs*. And in those postwar years, when they could feel the steady upward surge of the economy under them, it was surely only a matter of time before they could sell at a profit and buy a lot and have a brand-new house built. Ranch style, with everything electric. Meanwhile, Frank sweated and strained on this one. "Look at these," he would say, showing her double joists and old square nails hand-hammered by blacksmiths. "You don't see workmanship like this anymore. They built things *right*." His enthusiasm made her giddy. Despite her fear of heights, she climbed onto the roof during the big snow of '52 to help him shovel while the children tunneled in the drifts below. They sat around the oil stove in the living room – she loved that room: sixteen feet by twenty-four, the biggest she would ever have – while their boots and mittens dried. They ate cinnamon toast and drank hot chocolate and sang songs. Those were good times, Connie thought now as she vacuumed their bedroom – her first chance in days, with Frank out of it – and made the bed. But what had happened? The freeway thing was only part of it. He had worn himself out on this house. It was – let's face it, she thought – a shack. A dump. Just to make it weathertight had been an awful chore. Frank had to *fight* the house, just as he fought the railroad. And he got angry.

For Connie, finally, it wasn't the house that tried her patience, but the dirt. The back yard, with that bank, was hopeless. Nothing would ever grow there. It was just mud in the winter, dust in the summer. Dirty laundry without end. Not to mention the manure ... and though she sympathized with poor Thelma, did anyone *have* to have so many dogs and cats? *Listen to them now, yapping!* That was another subject – the neighbors. There were some fine people among them, like the Ordoñezes. Rough diamonds. For a while it had been fun to get to know them – people she would never have met in Oakland, on a hill of neat stucco homes and tidy lawns. It made her feel broader – and, again, adventurous. But some of her neighbors, even by the most charitable reckoning, were characters. And a few ... well, her father had a word for it. Two words: *Tobacco Road.* She had never read the book; she had no wish to read it. But it stood for everything she didn't want the children to grow up in. *Dirt.* Of course, they wouldn't be on Shasta Avenue forever – the freeway would make sure of that. But without any profit, would they be able to move anyplace much better?

No, Connie thought, an adventure was only temporary. It wasn't life. Life should be calmer and more comfortable. She deserved a better place, and so did the children. (Especially Tommy, who had been so terribly sick – infantile diarrhea – when he was three days old, and nearly died. Now he was strong and healthy, but slow. Brain damage, Dr. Reed thought. But how much, or what kind, nobody could say for sure yet.) And she missed having the other teachers – educated people – to talk to every day. Piling a batch of dirty clothes into the washer, trying to think about what to make for lunch – would Frank be back by then? In what kind of mood? Where on earth had he *gone?* – she made a promise to herself that she would carry out:

When the kids get a little older, I'm going back to work.

Once, after she visited the Ordoñezes, Fred had walked her out to the street. "Just want to let you know," he said. "Frank's a good man. He ain't like some I know. You see – " And Fred smiled and waved his hands, as if even to bring the subject up embarrassed him, though he had only good news for her. "– there's railroad men have two wives. One on the road, in Klamath Falls or Ashland. Maybe not *married*, but you know what I mean. They can get away with it for a while, the way the job is. What I mean is – " Fred smiled again and shook his head. "Frank ain't like that. You don't have to worry. He ain't the kind to be steppin' around."

This memory had always warmed her. It made her feel good about Fred – who hadn't *had* to say something like that – and her husband too; it confirmed her sense of safety. But now, in the shock of Frank's leaving so suddenly, it did the opposite. Men had secret lives, she thought. Some men, anyway.

She shivered.

Did Frank, after all?

No. Of course not.

And his nickname for her: "Mouse." She'd always thought it cute, and endearing. It meant he didn't care about the weight she'd put on, after three babies. Frank had always insisted that he liked big girls. But maybe, she thought now, there was a nasty dig to it, too – a reminder that she hadn't kept her figure.

Connie realized that there had been another reason why she'd shrunk from yelling at him from the porch. It was more than just a woman making a fool of herself where everyone could see and hear. It was worse: a *fat* woman yelling.

"I want to go fishing," Annie whined.

The girl had been saying this over and over. She knew something was wrong. Otherwise, why would she have clung to her mother all this time instead of running out to play?

"Maybe your dad will be home soon. I can't have you going down to the river alone."

But Annie just looked miserable.

"If your brother were just a little older...." *Tuna sandwiches*, Connie thought. *That's enough. And some Campbell's tomato soup.* She had no appetite herself. In fact, she was exhausted; first the argument and then Frank ... it was worn her out.

"Johnny's no good. He throws rocks in the water and scares the fish," Annie said. Then she brightened. "You think Clyde'll take me?"

"Maybe Clyde will. Let's hope."

5.

There's only one chance, Frank Hiller's old man in Sacramento had said. *That's what your grandpa told me, and it's true. Just one chance for the little man to get hold of some land. And that's when the frontier's just passed but things aren't settled yet. Just a handful of years at most. Because after that, the big boys get hold of it all, like they did back East or in Europe or wherever the hell you came from in the first place. Your great-grandpa came out West just in time and picked out a hundred and sixty acres right from under their noses, north of where the American River runs into the Sacramento. Grew corn, mostly. Had a peach orchard. It was good black bottom land. The best. We'd be landed gentry today if it wasn't for the goddamned SP and its freight rates. Oh, yes. That's what your grandpa told me. They squeezed him and squeezed him, and he finally had to sell out to the Farquhars, who were growin' hops all over that country, stringin' up vines, growin' hops to make beer with. They're doin' it still. Makin' a pile of money, I reckon. Because do you know who the Farquhars were? Pals of C.P. Huntington, that's who, who ran the railroad. They were just scratchin' each other's backs. And in those days, hell, son, the SP ran the Legislature too, and the newspapers. There wasn't anything your grandpa could do, though I know damn sure he wanted to. I was twelve then. He wanted to shoot those sonsabitches, and I'd've helped him if he asked.*

Frank, who was fifteen at the time, must have looked skeptical. The railroad, by then, was just a railroad.

You don't believe me, there's a book about it. Man with the same name as you wrote it. Frank Norris. The Octopus. *That's what he called the SP, because it had a whole bunch of arms that could rob you at the same time. Put it all down. It was a damn good book. Made up, you know, but true too.*

Frank found it in the Grant High School library. It was thick and musty and old-fashioned, slow going in places, but the old man was right. The railroad strangled the wheat farmers of the San Joaquin Valley and foreclosed on some and threw their belongings out into their yards. The farmers tried to fight back, but they were many little forces against a big one; they wavered and split, and they lost. A few got killed. There was a blacklisted railroader, Dyke, who had a chance to shoot the big boss, but his pistol misfired. It *had* to, Frank thought. There was no stopping the SP. Even at the end, when the big boss wandered into the hold of a grain ship and was buried alive, suffocated, by tons and tons of wheat pouring down on him from a chute – what a scene that was! – Frank understood that Norris was just trying to make people feel better. In real life, that never happened. The big bosses died peacefully in their sleep, as rich as ever.

Your grandpa never was the same. He had him a bunch of little strokes, one after another, and wasn't much good after that. Sometimes I think he should've *shot somebody. It wouldn't have turned out any worse for him. And it might have made ... hell, it might have made some of those sonsabitches* listen. *Just once.*

The old man, Frank knew, had vowed to get the farm back, but the best he could do was save for years and make a down payment on inferior acreage in the Del Paso Heights area – rockier land, too high to irrigate, good only for pasture. And then the Depression had wiped that out. Frank remembered only what was left: the house and a half-acre behind it where the old man still grew corn and his mother had a vegetable garden. And kept chickens. The old man had to work wherever he could and be grateful for it. He drove a Top Hat potato-chip truck, wearing a white shirt and a bow tie. His long brown hands – a farmer's hands – hung out of the shirt; he grew a mustache, as clownish as the tie, which Frank hated – it seemed to be a sign of giving up.

Your grandpa took me out there later to see those hopvines, see the land we'd had once and watch the Mexicans the Farquhars had working on it now. And he said: That's what the sonsabitches want. To turn us all into Mexicans. Stoop labor. He said: There's a time in every man's life, and it usually comes sooner rather than later, and never when you're ready for it. When it comes, nobody's gonna help you. I'm sorry, son, he told me. That's just the way it is. There's nobody but you to say if from here on out you'll be standing up or down on your knees.

Frank hadn't wanted to be a farmer. Just cleaning chickenshit out of those coops year after year was enough to sour him. (He didn't even like to eat chicken – though that didn't stop Connie from serving it.) But he wasn't cut out for indoor work, either. Not like his older brother, Ralph, who was a sissy, no good at sports, uninterested in girls, who took what money the family had and went to Sacramento State and studied engineering. For a while, after high school, Frank didn't know what to do. He'd outgrown wanting to be Dyke. *My gun won't misfire, by God. I'll plug him right in his fat belly.* It was 1937. All he could find was part-time work in a gas station, cleaning windshields and patching tires. And he realized soon enough that the old man hadn't given up, really. Like his own father, he'd had no choice.

Then Frank's friend and ex-teammate Bud Jones got the cockamamie idea to drive down to Arizona State in Tempe and work out for the coach and talk themselves into baseball scholarships. Bud claimed he'd written the coach, who'd said, "Sure, boys, come on down." So they piled into Bud's Model A Ford and, with twenty-five dollars to their names, headed into the desert. *My God! You thought the Central Valley was dry?* The Mojave was a whole different world. The Model A steamed on every grade. They scrimped on meals and slept in the car, the metal pinging as the heat left it, and by the time they got to Tempe they were sun-dazzled and dehydrated and in no shape to impress the coach anyway – not that he seemed to remember Bud's letter; not that he had any scholarships to offer. And even if he had, they couldn't afford to stay. They could barely make it back to Sacramento, chasing mirages up the two-lane concrete.

That was why Frank had ended up working for the SP a couple of years later. Like it or not, if you had nothing more than a high school diploma, nobody paid better than what used to be the Octopus.

# # # #

Now, suddenly, his time had come.

Frank would never tell anyone exactly what the Trainmaster said to him. Just a few words. Short and brutal. Like he wasn't a human being at all but just a piece of machinery that had slipped out of place and needed to be hammered back.

He couldn't lie down again because those words had stung as bad as the bruisc.

Sonsabitches.

And he had to get out of the house, finally, because he couldn't stand still.

Not with Connie running that damn vacuum in the living room, and Annie chattering along with her, as if what the Trainmaster had said didn't matter.

Nobody's gonna help you.

He'd told Connie the story, of course, about what had happened to the old man and *his* old man -- told her how he felt he was carrying both of them on his back, trying to make up for their losses; how the freeway thing had made him feel like just another patsy – a sucker in a long line of suckers, outsmarted by the big boys. He'd told her more than once. And she'd smiled and frowned and sympathized, but all he had to do now was step out of the bedroom with his clothes on and look at her face to see that she hadn't really heard. *And what could I expect?* he thought. *None of her people ever had a hard day in their lives.*

Then he felt he was falling.

He knew deep down that he was acting like a kid – he would be ashamed of himself later – but he was furious enough to push out onto the porch, enjoying her flurry of alarm. *Now, damn it, maybe you'll listen. Just once.*

Then gravity seemed to take over. Frank stumbled down the steps as if somebody had shoved him. He hauled himself up, grunting with pain, into the cab of the pickup. He could barely let his hind end touch the seat; leaning over the wheel with his head brushing the roof, he felt dizzy; his legs were at the wrong angles to work the pedals. But he couldn't stop now. *Just this once, by God.* Awkwardly, he kicked the engine into a roar, snapped the brake. Then the street in front of him led downhill, and he drove – never mind where he was going.

At the bottom of the slope, where the street forked, he saw two boys up at the edge of the woods, crouching, as if trying to sneak up on somebody.

Grissom's kids. Okies. *Tough little guys*, Frank thought.

Then he drove up the hill past the Grissoms' house and down the other side. He thought of his own son: how Johnny never met his eye. Tried too hard to please most of the time; then, if you just looked at him wrong, he made himself scarce. *Is it too late already?* Frank wondered, thinking of his brother, Ralph, who had that same washed-out look to his face, who had still never married. *Something's wrong with him*, Frank thought – though exactly what was wrong with Ralph, he would never come close to saying, even to himself.

Connie thought he was too hard on the kid. That was another bone he had to pick with her. Couldn't she see it was for Johnny's own good? *The world could kill you and not even blink.* Who would be there to help *him,* when his time came?

Nobody.

6.

Still, John had a gun.

It was a cap pistol from the local Sprouse-Reitz store. It wasn't as good as the Hopalong Cassidy pistol he'd gotten in Sacramento last summer, but that one had broken. He still had the holster, though. Black leather with thongs and a silver concho. He lay under the trees on the dead leaves and pine needles and acorns, thinking of the Weinstock-Lubin department store, around the corner from the Senator Hotel, just a block from the Capitol, where he'd ridden the escalators up and down while his parents were shopping. It had three floors and a mezzanine. The escalators were like stairs, but they moved all by themselves. The steps hummed up through gleaming metal teeth like a belt; then they separated into blocks and carried him smoothly, effortlessly, with a thrill in his stomach, as the rubber railings pulled his hands at exactly the same speed; then the steps flattened out again and threatened to drag him down through another set of metal teeth (he always felt a twinge of fright). He never got tired of it. Up and down. His parents – both had grown up in cities – smiled at him.

"You take care of that gun, now," his father said.

His mother added, "You have to remember, even toys aren't cheap these days."

"It's just like a real gun," his father said, "or tools. You take care of things, put them back in the right place, and they'll last."

"I will," John said.

But the gun broke anyway. He'd known it would, the moment his father told him.

Just like a real gun....

But it wasn't real. It was just a cap gun, and he was tired of cap guns. When he turned twelve, his father said, he could get a .22 rifle and go hunting – "if you learn to take care of it better than this." But even a .22 wasn't the same as his father's .30-06 deer rifle, or his double-barreled 12-gauge shotgun – those smooth varnished stocks and red-rubber recoil pads, the scope on the rifle, and the heavy, blued steel of the barrels, smelling faintly of oil and gunpowder.

A blue jay screamed above him.

He wondered if it was the same blue jay he'd shot with his BB gun on the hillside behind his house. Probably not. That one had just stood there, shifting its feet, on the dead, wirelike underbranch of a little fir. He'd zeroed in on it with his lever-action Daisy and squeezed the trigger. A burst of feathers. Horrified, he'd started to run forward ... and then seen the bird fly away, flashing blue and gray, apparently unhurt. So that he'd hardly had time to feel the horror before it changed into something else.

"Why didn't I kill it?" he'd asked at dinner, still disappointed.

"Well," his father shook his head, "you needed a little more ordnance there, I think. That's a pretty big bird for a BB gun. His breast feathers were too thick."

"His *feathers* stopped it?"

His mother said, "I don't think he should be shooting guns anywhere near the house. *Any* kind of gun."

"When I was his age, I was hunting rabbits out in the fields. Where all North Sacramento is now," his father said. "Didn't do any harm. Got some rabbits, too." And then, that rarest of blessings, he winked at John as if they shared a joke, and said, "Women."

# # # #

Now Freddie Ordoñez whispered, "What do we do now?"

"Just lay low for a while."

"They're comin', I think."

"They can't see us here. If we don't move."

Then a second blue jay screamed, in another tree, and the first answered. He thought he could hear the crackle of footsteps. Darn birds might give them away.

"They're comin'," Freddie said.

"Look," John said. "You hold 'em here, OK? Lay low and ambush 'em. Then I'll sneak around behind 'em."

Freddie rolled his brown eyes. He didn't like that either. In the movies, they knew, it was always the sidekick, like Gabby Hayes, who had to hold the horses and cover the hero while the hero sneaked around behind. *In a little while,* John thought, *he'll get too big to do what I say.*

"Cover me," John said.

He couldn't resist saying it. Turning to run up the trail, he looked back for a second at Freddie scrooched around a black oak tree: the way his black hair shone and his back was brown and smooth too, in the sunlight and the shadows of the leaves. He wished he had skin like that. If he did, he thought, he wouldn't have to feel naked, even when he was.

7.

At times like this, Connie Hiller always thought of her father. In the years after her mother's death, he had never failed to come into the girls' room in the evening and listen to them say their prayers. First the Lord's Prayer, then "Now I lay me down to sleep." They had closed their eyes to see him still in their minds, silhouetted against the doorway, a reassuring, solid bulk. He never missed a night, no matter how tired or busy he might have been. It was a comfort to her then, just as the memory of it was now. How well he understood them! (If she could only say the same for her stepmother, who was small and quick and excitable and sharp-tongued.) When they enrolled at Cal, he had taken Henrietta aside, and Connie two years later, and told them, "Whatever happens, keep your chin up. You're as good as anybody else."

Their motto.

They believed him. How could they not?

And she remembered George getting sick. That was in '43, not long after she had married Frank. The fever, the weakness, the poor boy out of his head, almost completely paralyzed ... her father and stepmother had needed Connie, because Henrietta was already pregnant and Wylie was shipping out soon with the Navy. So she went back to Oakland for the summer and helped care for George. They turned him over twice a night and rubbed his wasted body – his Adam's apple was so huge; black whiskers were just beginning to sprout on his chin – with mineral oil to prevent bedsores. He was sensitive to light and had to lie behind drawn shades. Meanwhile, Frank got a transfer to the Oakland Pier, loading baggage onto troop trains. That way he could spend two days a week with her, on average, in between trips to Klamath Falls and even Portland. It was hard on them – hard on their brand-new marriage, she thought now; they had no privacy in her parents' house – but what else could they have done? She had always loved George, and never more than in those dark weeks when she sat by his bed and moved his limbs to exercise them and read to him as if he were a child again. They all prayed, in their different ways. Frank liked her father, she knew, but also thought he was ... what? Bland, unemotional. But here was a man who had lost his wife and now might lose his son, and what could be finer than the way he kept steadily, gravely on as before? *Chin up.* Some of the modern wonder drugs weren't available then, but thank God they had sulfa. George didn't die. The strength in his body slowly came back – except for his left arm and right leg, which would always be weak. Not like little Jackpot Sykes up the street; George had maybe half their use still. He could walk, shuffling along, his shoulders tilted, and go fishing with Frank on the McCloud River or the Klamath or at Box Canyon here on the Sacramento, if someone helped him over the slippery rocks. To that extent, their prayers had been answered.

Still, George (an accountant now, at a shipping firm in San Francisco) had never been able to marry. *And he was such a handsome boy.*

Connie thought of how good Frank had been with him, how much pleasure it gave George to come north on those fishing trips. And she was able, for a while, to calm herself.

This was just a quarrel, she thought. It would pass.

Nothing remotely as serious as what had happened to George. Nothing every couple didn't go through now and then.

If only he gets back before they call his crew. And apologizes to Mr. Ross. And doesn't hurt himself any worse.

She smoothed her face, smoothed the front of her shirtwaist and knelt beside Tommy as he played with the blocks. They were educational blocks – a hollow wooden cube with holes in it, and blocks to fit those holes: a square, a triangle, a circle, a half-moon. "How's it going there?" she asked and nuzzled the close-cut top of his head, kissed him behind the ear.

He wiggled and made an impatient sound: "Ee-e-e!"

She bent closer. Sometimes the desire to teach was overwhelming, though she wasn't sure – maybe it was better to let him try on his own. "Do you know where that one goes?" she asked. He was holding the triangle, painted orange.

Tommy slid it across the top of the cube. He paused it beside the half-moon hole and looked up at her.

"Is that it?"

But something in her voice seemed to tell him it wasn't. He slid it on to the square hole and paused again. Tommy's gray eyes were unusually deep-set; a sudden gleam came from them, and she wondered for an instant if he was teasing her.

"Is *that* it?"

But maybe not, she thought, because he tried to push the block in and it didn't go. Then he slammed it down on the floor and glared up at her (just as Frank had glared from beside the truck) as if its failure to fit was her fault.

"Well, that's not the one, you see," Connie said patiently. "This one's got three sides. Where's the hole with three sides?"

"Tree side!" Tommy said.

"That's right. One, two, three. Where's the hole with three sides? Here, try again."

And maybe – *probably* – it was luck, she told herself, but this time Tommy not only slid the block over the triangle hole but had it lined up perfectly, so that it dropped through in a flash and rattled on the bottom of the cube.

Tommy looked up, astonished.

"That's *it!*"

Then he looked unhappy – pushed his lower lip out – as if he had somehow lost the block. As if he would cry any second.

"No, you did it! That's *right!*" It took Connie a while to convince him, tipping the cube over and showing him the orange block, safe.

"That's what you're *supposed* to do. You put it in the right hole and *bingo!* There it went."

It took her a while, but his grin, when it came, was dazzling.

"Oh, you're a sweet, sweet boy," she said. "And a smart one, too." *That other doctor, the nerve specialist, said you'll never learn to read, but what does he know?* And indeed Tommy would grow up to read quite well, though numbers would always be hazy to him.

Connie kissed Tommy again – he still had a little of that clean baby smell the others had lost – but he struggled away, reaching for another block: the circle.

"OK, Mr. Grumpy," she said. "See if I care."

She went into the kitchen and started cutting bread for sandwiches. The washer rumbled. Cleo scratched at the back door. Connie let her in; the dog nosed at her food dish – empty already – and lapped some water, then went on to the edge of the living-room rug, circled and lay down.

Annie was still following her mother – stuck on this going-fishing idea, like a broken record. "Here," Connie told her, handing down a stack of four plates. "Don't drop these. You can help set the table." The girl usually was willing to do this, but now she dawdled and scraped her feet. This nagged at Connie, like her own worries. The house was beginning to heat up. She could feel sweat prickle under her bra straps, at her waist. How much damage had Frank done, hanging up like that?

And why couldn't Mr. Ross be reasonable?

So that when she heard heavy, male footsteps on the front porch, she was flooded with relief.

"See! There's your daddy now. Just in time to eat."

She hurried to the door, not even thinking why Frank would bother to stop outside and knock, or why she hadn't heard the truck.

8.

It was better alone. John ran through the woods, first uphill, then across, at full speed, the holster slapping against his hip. He could duck the branches that whipped at him, hit a rock with each lunging step of his Keds, so he left no tracks. He knew these woods. All the branching trails – were they Indian trails? He didn't know, but he hoped so. Gary couldn't follow him here. Even the Japs or the Germans, if they ever came to Dunsmuir ... they'd be in for a surprise, he thought.

But he didn't run far. Before long he circled back behind a little ridge to where he could see the roof of his own house, below the clay bank. Then he lay down inside what he liked to call the fort – a four-sided hollow of cedar logs that somebody had cut and stacked and left there a long time ago. It was too small to be a real fort, he knew, but it *looked* like one – just as the trails looked as if they might have been Indian trails, before the white man's boots rubbed out the tracks of the moccasins.

Nobody could see him.

But he could see to both sides through the chinks in the logs, and down below, and even what he couldn't see – the bulk of the mountain behind him – he could feel pressing up against his body, like an unmoving wave. It was called Mt. Bradley; the top of it, the fire lookout, was five thousand feet above the town. Halfway up the trees ended; the rest was dark green manzanita – tall as a man sometimes. "Rip the clothes right off you, try to walk through it," his father said. "Much less drag a deer down." Across the canyon was Girard Ridge, not so high, with trees all the way to the top. The air was so clear and the sky so deep a blue – almost purple – that the sky and the trees, blue and green, seemed the same distance away, as flat as a picture; and the trees on the far side were just as sharp and bright a mixture of greens as the trees overhead. A breeze stirred their branches, but on the ground where John lay it was still and warm. The logs had a dry, rotten smell. Ants crawled in the gray twigs near his hand. A squirrel started to run down the trunk of an oak, saw him, and stopped upside down, flicking its tail.

He felt almost sleepy.

The town itself was invisible – so were the river and the railroad – but from time to time he could hear rushing water, or a big truck groaning down the grade from Mount Shasta City, or bulldozers working on the freeway – they sounded like huge animals chomping – or the metallic bang and echo of boxcars coupling in the yards. Nearer, a toy wagon rattled, a kid yelled –

Gary?

No, somebody younger. Some little kid.

He listened for Gary and Jimmy sneaking up the trail. That was the trouble with hiding in the woods. (He thought of real Japs and Germans again.) At first they didn't know where you were, and that was good, but after a while you didn't know where they were either....

And what about Freddie? He hadn't heard anything.

John held his breath. He could see just his own house, but he knew where everything in the neighborhood was, better than he would know any other place in his life – every crack in the sidewalks, every shortcut across a vacant lot, every picket in the fences he ran past with a willow stick, making a flapping noise like the playing cards they'd fasten with a clothespin to whirr against the spokes of their bike wheels. Like the noise a quail's wings made, his father said, flushing from cover.... It was all in his head like a map.

Just north of the Grissoms' house, on this side of the street, was a house with a tin roof and pale-blue asphalt shingles where, two summers ago, a new family had moved in. They had a daughter named Julie.

Julie Land. She was eight then, the same age as John. She had blond hair and green eyes; he'd never seen a girl so pretty. His stomach felt funny, just as it did on the escalators. She played in her front yard, by an apple tree, on top of a high concrete wall, so he had to look up at her. Her hair shone in the sun. She looked like a princess; he wanted to rescue her. (Maybe that was when he'd first had the idea of making a suit of armor.) But what – or whom – could he rescue her from? He tried to talk to her, and at first she'd been friendly, but later she wasn't so friendly anymore, and he (liking her just as much, but not knowing what else to do) had thrown green apples at her. It was almost funny to think about now. But when John was in high school, looking back, it would seem ominous – his first failure with girls in what had become a habit of failure, which he would understand no better than why he'd thrown those apples in the first place. Julie's father had come out into the yard and yelled at him, threatened to call the police. Before school started, even, they'd moved away.

Because of him?

John hoped not, but he couldn't help wondering.

Between that house and his own was Curly McPherson's house, set far back from the street in a grove of gloomy cedar trees. The sun never shone on it. Mr. McPherson didn't have a lawn; he just left the trees and the poison oak bushes underneath, with their telltale clusters of three shiny leaves that turned bright red in the fall. John wondered sometimes if Mr. McPherson was some kind of monster – a vampire, maybe – or a mad scientist who had a laboratory where, if a kid ever went in there, he'd do experiments on him.

"Don't be silly," his mother told him. "Curly's just a railroad man, like your father."

"But how come he never comes out?'

"He comes out whenever the crew dispatcher calls him, just like your father. At night or when you're in school. You just haven't noticed."

"But I watched," John said. "He never comes out. And nobody goes in, either."

"He's a bachelor. He doesn't have a family, so there aren't a lot of people going in and out." Then his mother – she was ironing – had smoothed out one of his sister's blouses on the board, set the iron upright with a hiss of steam, and smoothed out her face the way she did when she was serious. "Now, I'm not saying Curly isn't a little *strange*, maybe. Living alone can make you strange. But you kids shouldn't talk about him like that. Children can be very cruel that way, without even knowing."

"Aw, Mom – "

"Well, you *can*. And I don't want to hear you talk like that."

"He doesn't have a secret laboratory?"

"You have too much imagination." Then, no longer serious, she rubbed the top of his nead with her knuckles so he giggled. "Remember what I said."

On the other side of his house was Thelma Hoffman's house. She lived alone too – a middle-aged lady with a swollen face and swollen ankles who wore only slippers and a bathrobe, even in the daytime. Something had happened to her, his mother said, without telling him exactly what. Her family had been rich; she was the granddaughter of one of the lumber mill owners who had started the town of Weed. But Thelma Hoffman was poor. She sent local stories to the Sacramento Bee – John had heard her typewriter clacking – but his mother didn't think they paid her much, and he wondered how she found any stories to send, shuffling around in that old house with its gray, peeling paint and its smell. He didn't even want to go in there, the stink was so strong. She had six dogs, the kids figured – little, yappy dogs – and maybe two dozen cats. There was dog poop all over her yard. (That's what his parents called it. The solid stuff was poop and the water was pee. But other kids' parents taught them different words, like crap and taking a leak; that was strange. And then there were other words you weren't supposed to use.) It was all over John's family's yard, too, because there wasn't any fence – new, sticky poop and old poop that had gotten white and crumbly. Sometimes he shoveled it back into Thelma Hoffman's yard. Because although both yards looked the same – just bare clay, scooped out of the hill with a bulldozer – and his house was gray and peeling too, still, his family was different. Nothing bad had happened to *them*. His father was scraping the siding and planning to paint it a nice dark brown, with white trim; he'd bricked up the walk to the steps, built the porch in back and a retaining wall in front, and someday, he'd said, the place would look halfway decent.... *So there ought to be a line,* John thought. *No dog poop on our side.*

His mother felt sorry for Thelma Hoffman – called her "poor Thelma" and sometimes took her a batch of cookies – but she didn't feel sorry for the Sykeses, who lived in the far house, where Shasta Avenue ended. "Because they don't try," she'd told John in that serious voice. "It doesn't matter if you're rich or poor, so long as you try." Mr. Sykes had been in the Army and brought back a war bride from Italy. "Ten years in this country, and never learned to speak English," his mother said. Mrs. Sykes didn't often come out; she was fat and looked sleepy, or dazed; her face was dirty and so were the kids'; they had snot in their noses and rotten teeth. "I can understand being short of money, if he's out of work sometimes – though I don't know how hard he tries to *find* work – but there's no excuse for neglecting your children's teeth," his mother said. The oldest boy – there were two boys and a girl – had had polio; his left arm just hung from the shoulder, no bigger around than a broomstick. Yet the Sykeses were lucky, too; that same boy – they called him Jackpot, long for Jack – had been the first baby born in Siskiyou County that year. The family had received a big pile of gifts, his mother said. "So maybe God looks out for those who *can't* help themselves. I don't know."

On the other side of the street, turning back south, was Dr. Malevich's house, also his office: a sooty concrete building with little, high windows of frosted glass that you couldn't see through. "Like a Nazi pillbox," Gary said. Dr. Malevich's name sounded creepy, somehow, and he wasn't a real doctor, like Dr. Reed downtown. "He's a chiropractor," John's mother said. "People who don't know any better, he does something to their spine – massages them, I guess – and they feel better. For a while." From her voice he knew she didn't approve of Dr. Malevich either, and the way his house looked, it was easy to imagine *he* might have a laboratory inside where he did terrible things. But Annie had gone inside once and nothing had happened. That was after she'd gotten into a rock fight with Hughie Williams and smashed one of the headlights on Dr. Malevich's car. Annie had a good arm, John had to admit. Good as a boy's.

Their father had whipped her then, with a willow switch, so red welts stood out on her legs. "This isn't for the headlight," he told her, and then to John: "Listen up. It's because it could've been Hughie's *eye* instead. You could've blinded him. His folks could've sued us for every cent we've got."

"He started it," Annie said. She sounded choked, but she wasn't even crying much.

"I don't care *who* started it. No more rock fights."

Then he sent her across the street with a five-dollar bill. "Tell him if that's not enough, let me know." John watched her go, walking with her legs apart – they must have been stinging still – looking very small, with her auburn hair in a ponytail, holding the money very carefully in her outstretched hand; and at heart he'd wondered if he could be that brave. But Dr. Malevich hadn't done anything to her. He hadn't even taken the money.

Lucky.

Hughie and his little brother, Walt, lived opposite the Hillers, but their house faced the other way, toward Florence Avenue, which also was Highway 99. Their back yard was as big as other people's lots. It was mostly woods, with a clubhouse at the north end, in a cedar and willow grove, a wild blackberry patch in the middle, and then more woods, with a treehouse nailed between a couple of oaks. It was where most of the kids in the neighborhood played. Hughie had a sandbox next to the house; they filled it with water from a hose and floated toy boats in it – though sometimes Hughie's grandmother came out and told them to turn off the water; they were getting all muddy.

"Where's his mom and dad?" John asked once.

"Well, that's a long story," his mother said. "I don't know how much you can understand. But they got divorced. They don't live together anymore. And Hughie's grandmother ... well, they had a big fight. She didn't like Hughie's mother, and she and Judge Williams wanted to take the kids themselves. And they won."

John didn't understand. "Why didn't she like Hughie's mom?"

"She wasn't ... a lady," John's mother said. "I've probably said too much already. Don't talk to Hughie about it. It'd just make him feel bad."

South of the Williamses' back yard was the Knudsons' house, which was John's favorite in the whole neighborhood. Like most of the houses, it was old and needed paint, but it was three stories high and orange, with fancy carving – "a Victorian," his mother said, "like they built all over San Francisco after the earthquake in 1906" – with a tower on one corner. The round tower room had a roof like a witch's hat and curved windows that fit the walls. John wanted to live in that room more than anywhere else; wanted to look out those windows at the street far below.... But the people who lived there were the Lorenzos, who rented the top floor from Mrs. Knudson. The Lorenzos were strange too. The father was a little, dried-up old Filipino man who cooked in a Chinese restaurant down by the tracks. The mother was a white woman, big and fat, a head taller than her husband. The kids – a boy and a girl – didn't look like either of them. They had blue-black hair and pearly skin and dark eyes with long lashes, as if they both were girls. The boy, Paul, knew a lot of dirty stuff, even though he was younger than John. He was the one who had taught him the other words – the ones you weren't supposed to say.

"It isn't poop and pee," Paul said scornfully, so that John felt, for the first time, embarrassed for his parents. "It's shit and piss, man, that's what it *really* is."

Mrs. Knudson was a widow. She lived with a much older brother, Clyde Carter, who sometimes took John and Annie fishing. Her son, Ronnie, had stayed with them last summer after he got out of the Marines. The Marines, he told all the kids – sitting on the front lawn in his khaki pants, drinking a can of beer, stubble growing on his thin yellow face – were a hell of a lot tougher than the Army. "We do all the fightin'," he said, "and they just come along afterwards and take the credit." Thinking of Mr. Sykes, John figured maybe that was true. His mother said Ronnie was trying to "find himself" after being in the war in Korea. She sounded as if something was wrong with him. But Ronnie was OK. He made Gary, at least, want to join the Marines right away.

He sold John's parents his old bike for John to ride – fifteen years old, covered with dust, but heavy and strong, with big balloon tires. And one day he'd told the kids he'd show them how the Marines tied up prisoners so they couldn't escape.

"But first you try to tie *me* up," he said. "I'll get a rope."

He brought a clothesline. They wound it around and around Ronnie's long, lean body until he looked like a mummy. John wondered if he'd be embarrassed if he couldn't get loose – a Marine tied up by a bunch of kids. But Ronnie just grinned. Then he sort of shrugged his shoulders and the coils slid off him, like the coils of a Slinky walking down stairs.

"Now it's your turn," he said. "Any volunteers?"

John volunteered. Now he was the one who was embarrassed – Ronnie had got loose so easily. He vowed he'd get loose too. Maybe it *was* easy. He hoped so. But it turned out he didn't have a chance. Ronnie tied his hands behind his back, and then his feet, so tightly the rope hurt, and then tied his feet to his hands, so all John could do was wiggle on his stomach or flop on his side, like a trout somebody'd landed, while Ronnie stuck his face close to his, smelling of beer and cigarettes and sweat, and grinned.

"Lesson number one," Ronnie said. "Never volunteer for anything."

John hadn't liked that much, but still, Ronnie was OK. He'd gone away and gotten married. Maybe that was what his mother meant about "finding himself" – it meant finding somebody else.

Next, finally, was Freddie Ordoñez's house, across from the Grissoms'. The hillside was steep there – so steep that the street split in a Y, cars going south ten feet above cars going north, with a bank and trees in between. Freddie's yard was below the street, and a bridge ran from the sidewalk to the second floor, which was really the main floor. Mrs. Ordoñez, a quiet, pale woman, usually would be inside, making soup. Her kitchen shone. The smell of onions blended with the smell of ammonia; John didn't know which was to blame for her red-rimmed eyes, the downward turn of her mouth and the way she would sometimes pause in mid-sentence and sniff, her nose pinched, as if the smell had stung her nostrils and made her forget what she wanted to say. Mrs. Ordoñez even talked through her nose. That was because she was French, his mother said. Franch people talked through their noses. "But don't you make fun of her. At least she *speaks* English," his mother said, comparing her with Mrs. Sykes. In fact, his mother seemed to have a special liking and respect for Mrs. Ordoñez, and not just because of her housekeeping.

One day she'd told him why.

"In the war," she said, "in France, she was in the Resistance. Those were just people, ordinary people like us, who wanted to keep on fighting the Nazis after their army had surrendered. I don't know what Marie did – whether she sent messages and helped downed Allied airmen or what – but she was caught by the Gestapo. Those were the German police – but not like our policemen here; they were terrible people, they had concentration camps...." His mother sighed. "They tortured her."

"How?" John asked. He wanted to know, but then again he didn't.

"She didn't tell me everything. But she said" – and here his mother's voice was more than serious; it had a thrill to it, a catch in her throat, as if she wanted to make sure he never forgot this – "she said they put her in a bath so hot she fainted. And then, when she came to, they put her in another bath so *cold* she fainted. Back and forth, over and over."

"Oh," John said, a little disappointed.

"Think of it," she insisted. "How hot it would have to be to make you faint."

He thought of how hot bathwater could be – so hot he couldn't stand it. And that Nazi water must have been even hotter. He felt ashamed; his mother must have seen the disappointment in his face. And then, too, she might not be telling *him* everything – even as much as Mrs. Ordoñez had told her.

Because he remembered when she'd read him a Reader's Digest article about a Boy Scout who was arrested by the Nazis, somewhere in Europe. He'd carried messages on his bicycle. Maybe he was in the Resistance too. She'd read it with that same thrill in her voice, the same shining tension in her freckled face, as if she were reading "Evangeline" or "A Christmas Carol"; as if John ought to learn what being a Boy Scout meant, now that he was about to become one. His mother was nice, he knew – she wouldn't hurt anyone – but her ideas about what a boy should grow up to be were beautiful and fierce. *"They beat him,"* she read, and then stopped to explain: "And they aren't talking about like when your dad spanks you, They mean *really* beat. With whips or clubs, maybe.... *But the Scout was dumb."*

"Dumb?"

"He didn't tell them who'd given him the messages. He kept his oath."

"What happened to him?" John asked.

"They shot him. But he didn't tell."

So he figured they'd probably beaten Mrs. Ordoñez too, no matter what his mother said.

"Does she have any scars?" he asked.

"Outside, I don't know. She wouldn't show anyone, I'm sure.... But inside is another thing." His mother sighed again. "Fred told me – " That was Mr. Ordoñez: a short, stocky Mexican man, almost as dark as a Negro, who worked on the railroad too. With Mrs. Ordoñez so pale, that's why Freddie's skin was that nice medium brown. " – he was in the Army Medical Corps when we liberated Paris. That's how they met. He said she weighed less than eighty pounds when we rescued her. Just skin and bone.

"So that's why," his mother concluded, "you shouldn't ever make fun of her."

John promised he wouldn't. The next time he saw Mrs. Ordoñez, crossing the bridge to her house with a bag of groceries, he looked at her carefully. He saw no scars, but maybe they were underneath her loose, flowered dress. He offered to carry the bag.

"No, no, I don't need...," she said, surprised.

"Can I open the door for you?"

He followed Mrs. Ordoñez into the kitchen. She set the bag down on the table and turned to see him gazing up at her like a dog, with all the sympathy he could muster. He could feel it rise from his chest and pour out of his eyes, like some kind of science-fiction ray.

"What?" she said. "You want something to eat? A cookie, maybe?"

"No, ma'am. I just – " He wanted to tell her he was sorry about what the Nazi had done. But at the last moment he thought: *Maybe she doesn't want to be reminded of that stuff.*

"Why you look at me like that, with your mouth open?" She started to smile, but then – as if that ammonia smell had suddenly pinched her nose – her face turned suspicious. He could tell she thought he was one of those kids who *would* make fun of her. A smart aleck. "Eh? I do something to you? I sound funny, maybe? You think – "

"No, ma'am," he said desperately.

"You Mrs. Hiller's boy, no? She a nice lady. She no want you to make her ashamed. Go, go," she said, taking him firmly by the shoulders and shoving him out the door. "Go help your *maman.* Not me. You leave me alone."

# # # #

Now, lying inside the fort, John wondered what it would feel like to be tortured. Suppose he'd been carrying messages on Ronnie Knudson's bike and the Gestapo arrested him, dragged him down into their dungeons.

He listened: still nothing.

Keeping his head below the top log, he peeled off his shirt. He rolled it up and stuck it under his belt.

Then he lay down again, so that the twigs and pine needles poked his back. With satisfaction, he thought of the ants crawling under him too. Already, the sun seemed to be burning the thin, milky skin over his ribs; the shadows of the branches overhead marked his chest, as thin as whip-slashes....

He shivered.

Then, out of the corner of his eye, through a crack in the logs, he saw something move far below. John turned. It was his father, clumping stiffly down the front steps, wearing regular clothes instead of overalls. Where was he going? *Not to work.*

His father stopped, opened the door of the maroon truck and looked angrily back up – toward the porch, which John couldn't see. Then he got in, slammed the door and, after a second pause, drove off.

John remembered the argument then, and felt several things at once.

He was relieved, as always, that his father was going – he felt muscles relax in his shoulders, in his jaw, that he hadn't even known were clenched – but he was puzzled, too, by the slacks and the seldom-worn Hawaiian shirt, a tan-and-green pattern of palm branches. And it hurt to see his father struggle like that, just to climb up into the truck. As if he was crippled – for good?

He thought again of how Mr. Grissom had tossed the toolbox.

How can Dad beat him like this?

9.

It wasn't Frank. It was Clyde Carter.

His wire-rimmed spectacles gleamed in the shadow of the porch. He carried a bamboo fishing rod and a wicker creel; he wore a khaki canvas vest with pockets in it, full of jars of salmon eggs and split shot and other items Connie could only guess at. A dozen trout flies hung from his shapeless canvas hat, and he'd folded a pair of rubber waders over his shoulder. Clyde was old – almost seventy – with skin all flaked and spotted and stained by the weather. He didn't smile – he rarely did. But he was just the man Annie wanted to see.

"On my way down to the bridge," Clyde said, "and I thought I'd see if any of these youngsters...."

"Fishing!" the girl shrieked, and ran to get her child-sized rod.

"Johnny's out somewhere," Connie said. "I don't know...."

"Never mind *him,*" Annie said. "Let's go!"

"But don't you think you should – "

"Let's *go!*"

"Hold your horses, young lady. You haven't had your lunch yet." To Clyde she said: "Would you like to come in? Can I get you something?"

Clyde waved the suggestion off.

"You sure? Even a glass of water?"

"Plenty of water down there," Clyde said.

"Well, I suppose that's true. Just wait a minute," she said to Annie, "while I make you a sandwich, at least." Connie returned to the kitchen and put the fourth plate back into the cupboard. She cut the bread, spread on tuna and celery and tomato and mayonnaise, wrapped it in waxed paper and brought it out. All the while, Tommy watched them. He had let the blocks spill and followed Cleo when she got up lazily to greet Clyde. "But how are you going to carry it?"

"Plenty of pockets," Clyde said, patting his vest. He smiled then, a little.

"Well, that's true too. You be careful, now," she told Annie.

"I'll take good care of her."

"I know you will."

"I'll bring her back by ... say, two at the latest."

The girl was dancing with impatience, but Clyde waited a moment longer; Connie could see curiosity in him – his eyes slid toward the bedroom.

"How's Frank?" he asked.

"Oh, he's doing better," she said. "He's starting to move around now."

"Good. Glad to hear it."

Chin up.

10.

She was a peach, Frank Hiller had thought.

Just hanging there, full of juice, waiting for somebody to pick her off the branch, like one of the big freestones that grew on the tree in his back yard in Del Paso Heights. (Grafted from the original stock in his grandpa's orchard, they said – though you didn't see freestones so much anymore; the canners preferred clings.) A peach. Just hanging there, with the blush and fuzz on her, coppery hair and a prim expression that couldn't fool anybody who bothered to look. He'd come off the South End Pool from Red Bluff – a passenger run, for a change, so he'd worn the blue uniform and the silver-lettered brakeman's cap instead of overalls – and there she was, at the Red Cross table with the coffee urn and boxes of doughnuts, and a line of soldiers in front of her. Frank didn't mind the soldiers. They'd be gone tomorrow; he wouldn't. And neither would she – this Miss Constance Weldon. A peach. Almost *too* ripe from hanging there so long; almost ready to drop off the branch without anybody reaching for her. Built like a brick shithouse (Frank would never tell her that, of course) and unaware of it. Well, maybe a little. She knew just enough to keep her curves covered up. But she had no notion, he was sure, of what those curves were *for* – which made her irresistible. A peach. The kind of girl you were *happy* to take home to mama. A nice girl – a thoroughly nice girl – with a college degree, no less. Frank marveled at his luck. How come nobody else had picked her off? Guys must have been blind. Either that, he could come to think, or she had gotten them, somehow, to share her own blindness. So that those curves, if she didn't see them herself, didn't exist.

But she didn't fool him.

Hot damn.

Still, Frank thought now, after a dozen years, he'd been perfectly capable of fooling himself. Oh, yes. Maybe those other guys had seen something he hadn't – though if they hadn't married Connie Weldon, how could they know? It took a while to sink in. He'd thought Connie was shy, and she was, in a way. She had trouble disciplining the high school kids she taught. (As far as he was concerned, by taking her out of the classroom he'd done her a favor.) She didn't like to raise her voice, and even when she did, she didn't sound as if she meant it. Those teen-agers could tell. But what Frank hadn't seen at first was her stubbornness, her quiet insistence – bred into her, he thought, in that mission-style stucco house in Oakland, where only her stepmother raised *her* voice and the light always seemed dim and churchlike and there was hardly a speck of dust anywhere – that she knew what was right, what was proper, what was in good taste. Or maybe she got it from Cal, along with her diploma. As if that framed piece of paper with the fancy print on it meant she was smarter than he was, or knew more – not just that her family had more money.

Anyway, Connie *judged* things. And people. Every moment of every day, it seemed, she was passing judgment on somebody – on Dr. Malevich for being a quack and Ed Sykes for being a lazy bum (which he was); on Dunsmuir for being a backwater (which was true too, but still); and most of all on Frank himself, for his bad temper and dirty habits, for muddling through all the work he did on the house, for not being a crackerjack plumber like her father or an electronics whiz like her brother-in-law, Wylie Stone. She'd set out to improve him, and she never let up. Not that she'd order him to do this or forbid him to do that. Not Connie. That wasn't her way. She'd just look pained and long-suffering and tolerant. She *tolerated* it if Frank smoked or took a drink once in a while, but she wished he'd quit. Oh, yes. She *tolerated* it if he went hunting with Bob Chapman, but she thought by now he should have outgrown the need to camp out with other boys and come back unshaven and smelling of smoke, with something bloody and disgusting in the truck – something she'd have to cook, even if nobody particularly wanted to eat it.

And it wasn't the blood either, as you might expect. It wasn't the killing. That didn't bother her. Connie would help pluck the ducks and geese and even – a trick she'd learned from Bob's wife – melt paraffin in a saucepan and dip the birds in it and store them in the freezer. That way they kept for months. And when she wanted to roast one, she'd just peel off the wax and the pinfeathers with it. Neat. She would cook venison, though chewing that leathery stuff made your jaws ache. No, with Connie it wasn't the hunting. It was Frank's going away to do it – as if all those hours he spent on the trains and in Klamath Falls or Ashland weren't enough. "Do you *have* to?" she would ask, not expecting him to answer – for how *could* he answer? He was in the wrong. Somehow, with Connie, he was always in the wrong. *Togetherness* she wanted. That was fine. That was dandy. It was just .... *No, I don't have to,* he thought, *but by God, I* want *to.* And why? *Because without it ... without a little fun ... it would be like eating potatoes every day, nothing but potatoes, like some of my mother's people had to do back in Ireland in the old days. Surviving. But not living.*

"Don't you enjoy being with us?" she would ask. "After all – "

"Sure I do," Frank would tell her.

But the truth was, he thought, there was a *deal.* A deal they'd made when they got married. And Connie had reneged on it.

He thought about it in cabooses and in hotels at the other end of the line. He thought about it walking the trains at night, under the stars. He thought about it when business was slow and his crew wasn't called for days at a time and he sawed and hammered on the house to distract himself from the lack of money coming in. He thought about it when business was crazy and he hardly had eight hours to sleep, any time of night or day, before they called him again. (The kids *had* to be quiet then.) He thought about it when he'd "died on his sixteen hours," as they called it – union rules said you couldn't work any longer at a stretch than that. So a crew that had "died" waited in place to be relieved and rode back to town on a passenger train, often too tired to sleep, their minds clicking away as relentlessly as the wheels underneath. Most of all, he'd thought about it in '44 and '45 when he was trying to enlist and get off the railroad and into the war like Wylie, who had been in some of the naval fighting at Leyte Gulf. He thought about the deal – the promises he and Connie had made to each other. Unspoken but no less binding than the vows they'd stood up and made in church.

I'll take care of the outside of the house. You'll take care of the inside. I'll fix the cars. You'll take the kids to the doctor. I'll work at a hard and dangerous job; that's OK. I'll bust my back, because this is war too – the war every family fights on its own to survive, and to do a little better than survive.

Look at Tommy, Frank thought. All Connie saw was the cute little guy he was now. But what would happen ten years from now when Tommy put his hands on some girl because he didn't know any better? People in Dunsmuir would lynch him, crucify him. A small town like this had no mercy. The only hope was to put the fear of God into the boy, so that he never, never touched a girl. If that hurt him, so be it. It would save him from getting hurt much worse.

But if I bust my back, by God, then you ought to....

There had been a time, not just after the wedding but a little later, before they went down to Oakland to take care of George, before Johnny came along and then Annie, before Connie put on weight and never lost it. A time when her clothes came off and she no longer felt ashamed and awkward, when those curves were bared for Frank to see – when she kissed him back, kissed him hard, and seemed to mean it. All those *noises*. The *smell* of her. Three times a day they made love, if they could. Connie would get up in the middle of the night – whenever he came home from a trip – and fix him something to eat. All the barriers between a man and a woman were down. Things between them were ... he shied away from the words, because it wasn't *about* words. Tender, trusting. Why couldn't it have stayed that way? What put the barriers back up? Frank thought of his mother, disappointed over the loss of the farm in Del Paso Heights, not blaming the old man out loud but blaming him anyway, for sure; he thought of the old man's baffled face, of those long brown wrists hanging out of the white shirt. Had the same thing happened to *him?* Frank couldn't ever ask. And he couldn't blame Connie, really, and not be in the wrong again. It took a lot out of a woman, having a baby. Oh, yes. He'd seen it. Once she had the kids, she couldn't get up at ungodly hours to cook for him anymore. He understood that. And it was natural for her to put on a few pounds. *Hell, we all get old.* But it wasn't the weight, really, though she might not believe him. She was still a pretty woman. It was just that....

He still wanted it. What they'd had.

That was the deal.

Not *togetherness,* damn it, but the real thing.

And it was the one thing you couldn't ask for Frank knew. You couldn't beg. You couldn't say a single goddamn word.

All you could do was wait. Wait for Connie to change her mind, to feel a little of the old itch herself – though that had hardly happened at all in the last few years. Wait for her to remember: *That's what it's all* for. *All of this....*

He hadn't fooled around, by God.

And if he lost his temper now and then, hell, he'd been tired. Exhausted. *You have no idea how often I've just stood there and gritted my teeth and taken it. I haven't yelled at you. I haven't slapped you around, and there's more men do that to their wives than you can believe. I could name you names, right in this town.*

When I stop talking and walk away, Frank thought, *that's the absolute, level best I can do right then. Don't you realize that?*

I'm trying to tell you something. Is it so hard to figure out?

I want you to act different. Be *different, like you used to be. Stop all this complaining about stuff that isn't important. Then everything will be fine.*

But that was the problem, Frank thought. *You have no idea.* Connie insisted on comparing him with her father, a man so calm he hardly had a pulse.

And as time had gone by and Frank looked around him, he'd seen that other men were in the same fix. Maybe not Fred Ordoñez; Fred always seemed happy, though Marie had a sour look to her. She had a right to it, poor woman, after what she'd gone through. Maybe she *couldn't* smile anymore, even if she wanted to. Fred didn't seem to mind. But Frank couldn't name more than two or three other men he knew who looked as if they still had what they'd gotten married for – and once you saw that, he thought, it made more sense why they acted as mean or stupid as they did sometimes. Why they got drunk or picked fights or made life miserable for the younger guys. It was something that nobody talked about but everybody knew: a grim joke. Old Frank Norris knew it. He kept writing about how *forces,* not wishful thinking or morality, moved people. Blind forces, like Nature's need to get more babies born. You got married thinking it was one thing when it was really something else, simple and brutal, that had nothing to do with you. An old guy like Will Jamison – you couldn't go to him and complain about how things were at home, except in the most general way. *Hell fire, son*, he would say. *What do you think this is?*

A joke.

Like getting hit in the ass.

11.

Years from now, Connie Hiller would read newspaper stories about child molesters and murderers and feel uneasy about having let Annie go fishing alone with Clyde. What could she have been thinking of? How well did she know Clyde Carter, really? It appalled her. The things that could happen to little girls.... *It was a simpler time*, she would tell herself. *More innocent. People didn't think about such things*. But was that true? People might not have *talked* about them so much, but weren't there just as many evildoers around in those days? Probably, she thought. Yet Clyde, as far as she knew, had never done anything bad. Annie had had a wonderful time. If Connie had been more suspicious – a better mother, maybe – she would have deprived her daughter of that, and Clyde too: the pleasure that young and old could have together.

What was the answer? She didn't know.

Today she was relieved to see Annie and Clyde go off together – the girl had been pestering her so. But once she was alone in the house with Tommy and the dog, the silence seemed to close in on her. She almost wished she had one of those television sets that her brother-in-law, Wylie, sold and repaired in Richmond. An "idiot box," Henrietta called it. But it would be something to listen to, at least. The nearest stations were in Redding and in Medford, Oregon, more than fifty miles away, and the mountains around Dunsmuir blocked all reception. She would have to wait a few more years for cable to be laid. Meanwhile, there was only one radio station: KWSD. Weather reports and polkas and sermons – each one beginning *The cosmic hour has struck, loved ones!* – by the widow of the founder of a religious sect that had bought the old Shasta Springs resort north of town and believed that little people, Lemurians, lived inside Mt. Shasta.

"Come on," she told Tommy and went out onto the porch in hope of a breeze. It was getting hotter.

She sat in the shade in a folding chair while he ran down the steps. "Don't go into the street!" she called. Tommy had been slow to walk – as with everything else – but now he was a regular monkey. He had a yellow toy bulldozer with a blade that moved up and down. He moved dirt with it, as he'd seen the real bulldozers doing. He pressed the back of his left hand to his mouth and trembled. He made noises – and not just bulldozer noises, either. If she listened carefully, she could hear him invent companions, voices that noted his hard work and cheered him: "Yay, Tommy!" His hand had an ugly callus already. It embarrassed her when other people saw it – saw him lost in his little made-up world – and then she felt ashamed of being ashamed. Wasn't this play-acting a sign of something? *Don't tell me there isn't a mind in there,* she'd think. Some parts of him had to be undamaged. But which?

Cleo followed him. She sniffed at the dirt he'd plowed up, sniffed at him, licked him behind the ear. Tommy giggled.

Such a good dog. *She seems to know,* Connie thought. *She knows he's a baby, he's special, she has to be extra patient.*

Just after Tommy was born, and before he got sick: this was Connie's secret. Her memories of her father she shared with Henrietta and George. This was hers alone. Tommy was her biggest baby – nine pounds, six ounces – and had caused her the most pain. The first baby she'd had not in Oakland but in the little hospital in Mount Shasta, with Dr. Reed attending. It had been early September. Just as hot. A forest fire was burning to the north, near Black Butte, and smoke blew into town. Ever since, when she smelled a forest fire, she remembered what it was like to lie in the recovery room, so exhausted that she seemed to float on the bed, to drift with the acrid smoke. She floated, she felt, into a starry night sky, to the farthest end of the universe. She could see everything, and she understood that everything was all right. She sighed and relaxed (in the body she'd left behind) all the way down to her bones. *Why do people worry so much? Why do we struggle? It's all so simple.* Connie remembered thinking those words. They were what God meant to her now – not the church service every Sunday, though she went.

It was strange, Connie thought. To have had such a feeling just once ought to last a lifetime. She shouldn't ever worry again. But she did.

Where *was* Frank? He'd never done anything like this before.

Hunting for another family, maybe.

She could still see him hobbling down the steps, hear the slam of the truck's door, feel the outraged numbness spreading over her face.

The dogs next door barked; Cleo pricked up her ears. Kids shouted somewhere down the street. Johnny?

And she found she couldn't sit still anymore. "Come on," she told Tommy. "Let's heat up the soup. Do you want a banana, like your sister?"

"Banana!"

"You want one?"

"Yes," Tommy said.

"What's the magic word? Yes, *please*."

Before fixing lunch, Connie called the crew dispatcher. No, the switchboard girl said, Frank wasn't there, and he hadn't stopped by. His crew was fourth out. Maybe they'd be called as soon as dinner time. But you never knew for sure.

12.

Driving downtown, Frank felt as if he were kicking free of Connie and lunging at the Trainmaster all at once.

He imagined their faces recoiling as he smashed them. It felt sick – a shame and regret deep in his gut – but it felt good, too: this letting loose at last.

Falling.

The pickup bucked as he tried to work the pedals standing. His head bumped against the roof; the backs of his legs ached. But when he sat down for just a second – just brushed the upholstery – the pain of the bruise jerked him back upright. Sweat ran into his eyes. He was on Florence Avenue now, Highway 99, heading south, and the town *looked* different as he squinted and blinked at it – the way once, when he'd been hit in the head playing football at Grant High, the whole world turned a bright pale aqua color and he heard ... not birds tweeting, like people said, but a kind of tinny music. Dunsmuir looked like a place he'd never seen. No, that wasn't it, Frank thought. Like a place he'd never see again, not the way he used to.

Because what he was doing now would change it forever.

And change *him*.

For maybe the last time, he drove past the elementary school and the Texaco and Union gas stations. It was a small town. *Damn* small. Already he was plunging down the hill into its center – between Dr. Reed's office and the Owls Club and Littrell's auto parts and Mannee's pharmacy on one side and the California Theater, the Masonic Temple and the Sprouse-Reitz on the other. He groped for the clutch, the brake. The truck jerked again. Nothing he saw looked real. All that mattered was this sick, terrible pressure inside him and the momentum of his fall. He screeched to a stop at the corner as one of Connie's teacher friends – he knew the woman's name, but he couldn't remember it now to save his life – crossed in front of him. She waved. Frank waved back. Why not? Her dress had pink flowers on it. Shiny grease spotted the asphalt where her feet stepped. None of it was real. He turned left on Pine Street by the Bank of America and plunged again. Down, down, the lumber and bricks in the bed of the truck rattling. Out of the corner of his eye he saw his neighbor Ignacio Lorenzo climbing the sidewalk to the bank. Little, skinny, coffee-colored old Ignacio, grabbing a break before the lunch crowd showed up at Motto's, where he cooked Chinese. And even at this moment, Frank thought the same thing he always thought when he saw Ignacio: *Better not let that woman of yours ever get on top, pal. Because there won't be anything left of you but a grease spot.*

Just a block to the bottom: then the street ended. Frank crossed Sacramento Avenue. He tried to park against the retaining wall and iron-pipe railing of the lawn between the crew dispatcher's office and the depot. There were benches, a clock on a tall pole, a fountain where speckled trout swam. But by now the sweat in his eyes was stinging him half blind. He braked too late. The front wheels hit the curb; Frank's nose hit the rear-view mirror. He yelled. Then the truck rocked back and he fell against the seat, tasting salty blood, and yelled a second time – like an echo – at the pain in his rear end. He lurched back up, yanking the handbrake. The engine shuddered and stalled. He picked up a rag from the floor and tried to wipe his eyes, but this only seemed to drive the sweat in deeper. He was crying.

Frank got out.

All this time, he realized, he'd been yelling at Ross in his head:

Didn't your mama teach you right? Huh? Didn't she tell you not to be an asshole?

Who the hell do you think you are? God?

You think you can do anything you want to people and you'll always get away with it? Huh? You don't think anybody'll ever fight back?

Well, this time....

But now he was dabbing at his eyes *and* his nose, dribbling blood onto the stupid Hawaiian shirt he'd pulled out of the closet at random, trying to suck blood back into his nostrils while he flooded the stinging out of his eyelids with tears. Neither worked. To get to the Trainmaster's office he had to go down around the front of the depot and up a flight of stairs. But he couldn't *see.* He had to close one eye at a time while he squinted out of the other for a second or two, then switch eyes. Everything was wavery splinters of light: the turntable where one of the new diesels, painted red and orange – a passenger engine for the Shasta Daylight – was swinging slowly to line up with its stall in the roundhouse, like a bullet in a revolver clicking into place to be fired; the footbridge over the tracks to the engine shops; the two-story depot, yellow with brown trim; a couple of men in overalls lounging by the crew dispatcher who had looked up as the truck slammed the curb and now gawked at Frank as he stood there with blood and tears running down his face. He dabbed again with the rag – but the rag was filthy.

Was that Jamison?

Nothing had gone as Frank had hoped. No way he could burst into Ross' office now and face that icy little man behind the desk when he looked like an idiot who'd been in a bar fight. Because even if he could haul himself up those stairs – and the bruise was hurting like hell – wouldn't Ross just turn it against him?

You made it this far, Hiller, haven't you? And you want me to believe you're in such bad shape? Well, I'll tell you something. What you don't want is for me to run out of patience.

Ross wouldn't blink, either. Even though he was five-seven, tops, and pushing sixty.

The Trainmaster scared Frank a little. That was the truth.

But Frank didn't let himself realize that yet. He just thought of how ridiculous he looked. *All this blood. Jesus.* Nobody would let him get anywhere close to Ross without stopping him and asking questions. He struggled again to see. Yes, he thought, that was Jamison coming out onto the porch of the crew dispatcher, lighting a cigarette, and he recoiled from that as fast as his tires had bounced off the concrete.

Mindless.

Frank jumped back into the truck. He started it, backed up with a squeal of rubber, yelled again at the pain and headed south on Sacramento, willing the big hunk of maroon steel to vanish into thin air like a mirage on the Mojave, willing Jamison not to see it. That seemed possible. It was still like that moment on the football field: the pale-green tint of shock, the music. None of it real, including himself. So maybe he could escape. He passed the pool hall and Byrd's barbershop and Motto's. But then, as if the truck were steering itself, he turned right on Cedar Street, and somebody else he knew was standing at the entrance to the S&J Market – Dino Bastiani, wearing his butcher's apron. Dino waved. A good guy. Again Frank waved back. *Who next?* All these people seemed to be reaching out to grab him, hold him back. The street rose steeply to City Hall. One of those godawful Dunsmuir grades where you had to ride your clutch at the stop sign. His hamstrings screamed. His nose still dripped blood. The Commercial Garage, across Florence, was dead ahead – and was that Charley Grissom he saw in one of the service bays, setting down a tool to look? *Damn.* Frank wrenched the wheel, heading back north.

Escape. That was it.

What the hell had he thought he was doing, trying to punch Ross out? He'd end up in jail.

Screw him. *Just get out of here, by God.*

Leave this town.

Now.

Why not?

And once again Frank had that sick, thrilling feeling in his gut. Once again Dunsmuir faded and became unreal. He passed Tallerico's shoe repair and Lockart's hardware, the Travelers Hotel and the Big Liquor, the bakery and the flower shop – Connie's friend just turning into it. That pink-flowered dress. Jesus. Did she wave *again?* Had she gotten a good look at him, bleeding like a stuck pig? He gunned the engine to take the hill past the theater. His legs cramped even worse. Then he glanced down and saw the needle of the gas gauge bouncing on empty. He wasn't going anywhere like *that*. At the top, he pulled into the Texaco – but the man who owned it now was his old shortstop, Brian Behnke, and Behnke himself was standing at the pumps.

"Fill her up," Frank said. Still dabbing at his face with the rag.

"Jesus, what happened to *you?*"

"Never mind," Frank said, but he stumbled on the running board trying to climb out, and Behnke caught him by the arm.

"You'd better clean up. Use the men's room. Holy shit." Behnke grinned. "What's the other guy look like?"

"No other guy." Though he *had* been in a fight, in a way.

"Ran into a door, huh?" Behnke had put on weight since his playing days. He never tanned, just turned red – his jowls, the tops of his ears under the cap with the Texaco star. He eyed the Hawaiian shirt. "I like the style anyway, bud. It's colorful."

"Check the oil, too, why don't you."

"Hey, don't bite *my* nose off."

"Sorry, man. I'm just...."

If Frank thought he was sweating before, it was twice as hot in the narrow metal stall, smelling of urine and disinfectant. A steam bath. Water popped from his skin. He pulled out a wad of paper towels. There wasn't just blood on him but grease – from the rag. What a mess. The shirt was ruined. Splotches of blood drying on it like scabs. He ran water and poured gritty Boraxo soap into his hands and scrubbed himself as best he could. His nose was cut on the fleshy part outside one nostril; more blood seemed to be coming from inside. He wet some towels, folded them, tilted his head back and tried to stop the flow with pressure. He closed his eyes to keep the sweat out. He could hardly breathe – and how could blood clot when he was swimming in his own juice?

Frank had time, standing there, to remember. Too much time.

Had it been Jamison there at the crew dispatcher, or somebody else – a handy excuse to run? Dazed and humiliated, he couldn't be sure.

Either way, his gun had misfired.

Just like Dyke's.

And it came to him, as he left the restroom, that for five whole minutes he'd forgotten about the bruise. Did that make Ross right?

Damn.

Once he remembered about it, of course, it hurt like crazy. He limped over to Behnke, who had the hood of the truck up. "You're a quart low," Behnke said.

"Ten-forty, then." Frank turned and went to the machines at the front of the station. He bought a Coke and two packs of Chesterfields.

It seemed almost cool outside. Sweat had stuck the shirt to his ribs. He opened the Coke and drank it, and by then the hood had been lowered. Behnke tossed the empty oil can into a drum and wiped his forehead with a rag as dirty as Frank's. Behnke had eyebrows so blond you almost couldn't see them. He gave Frank a different look – not amused, simply curious.

"I heard you got hurt up here," he said, waving to the north. "Fred told me."

At least he didn't say *hit in the ass.*

"Yeah."

"As bad as he said? You shouldn't be out walkin' around, bud. Much less leadin' with your schnozz like that."

"Tell *them,*" Frank said bitterly. "*They* think I should."

Behnke perked up at that. He wanted the story. And Frank discovered that he wanted to stay there and tell it, even though Behnke usually wasn't much of a listener. He paid for the gas and oil: only eighteen dollars left in his wallet. Another obstacle. Should he go back to the bank? Ten minutes ago he'd seen his chance and taken it, appalled and thrilled by the enormity of his crime, knowing that if he paused even a second too long he would chicken out on that too. He'd seen an opening, like a halfback spotting a momentary gap in the line, and bolted for it. But all it took was an empty gas tank, a little soap and water – he still had to hold his nose up so it wouldn't start bleeding again – and something like sympathy....

Damn.

He had just enough momentum left to drive off and leave Behnke unsatisfied.

Down in the canyon, a train made a mournful sound.

Frank knew he ought to stop at home. Change his clothes, pack, collect his guns and tools ... hut he knew he couldn't. He would be trapped there by having to face Connie and the kids again. *Keep moving.* But where, for God's sake? He turned east off Florence and bumped down a steep little street under a dark tunnel of trees, beside a bank of moss and ferns that never dried out. He crossed the tracks after the caboose of a northbound freight passed by. Eric Riemersma's crew. That meant Jamison's was third out. Two other crews would be called on the North End Pool before Frank had to make himself available. (*Had* that been Jamison? The more Frank tried to remember, the more he doubted it. A mirage....) He rattled over a bridge and turned north on River Avenue, where the green wall of Girard Ridge came right down to the water.

Nobody around. Frank parked beside the river. It was shady here. A good place to hide for a while and try to think.

The bruise stung angrily now. His nose throbbed. He got out and leaned against the truck and lit a cigarette, looking west toward the big highway bridge.

After a while, he noticed an old man and a boy come through the willows and start fishing on the far side, maybe a quarter-mile away.

No, not a boy. Frank recognized the red-checked shirt, the black cowboy hat.

Annie.

He stood and watched her as she sat on a rock and watched her line. She never looked his way.

He lit more cigarettes. The breeze off the river eddied the smoke.

The noon whistle blew.

By then he'd been crazy, he would figure, for a little more than an hour.

13.

John didn't see Clyde Carter come, or see him and Annie leave. He was lying on his back in the fort again, eyes closed, thinking of that trip to Sacramento when he'd gotten the cap gun. He'd gone to the dentist there, too – Dr. Chenoweth, who didn't believe in using novocaine. "Unless it's something serious," his mother said before they left Dunsmuir. "I agree with him. Drugs are dangerous. You shouldn't use them unless you have to. *You* don't need anything for just some little cavities."

John looked at her dubiously.

"You aren't a crybaby, are you?" she teased.

"No."

"So there. *I* don't use any novocaine, and it doesn't hurt me much."

"Can't we go to the dentist here?"

"Dr. Chenoweth has taken care of your father and me for years. Think of this: when I was a girl, they didn't even *have* novocaine. You just had to be brave.... Anyhow, we trust him. He's a good dentist. And since we're going to be down there anyway...."

But it *had* hurt, as he'd known it would. It was as close to being tortured as anything he could think of, and he hadn't been brave at all.

Dr. Chenoweth's office was in a nine-story building – a skyscraper – and the elevator that lifted John up to the seventh floor seemed to leave his courage behind in the lobby with his stomach. He remembered the waiting room with its shiny brown leather chairs, its medicinal smell and the view out a window to the blank brick wall of another building, with a sign painted on it: HOTEL SACRAMENTO.... Then he was in the dentist's chair, with wads of cotton in his mouth, and tubes sucking, and a trickle of water in the basin (like blood, he thought); and the drill buzzed and whined into a hot point of pain while little bits of his teeth (it felt like) dropped on his tongue and the very air inside his mouth smelled and tasted like scorched iron; and Dr. Chenoweth's face, with its glasses, its clipped gray mustache and its high, tanned forehead – as smooth as the leather on the chairs – showed no emotion except for a faint impatience.

"I can't do it while you're moving so much," he'd say. "You want me to drill a hole in your tongue?" And finally, laying down the drill with a sigh: "OK, let's take a break. I'll see somebody else for a while.... You can spit."

So John would be left alone, sometimes in the dentist's chair, sometimes back in the waiting room, where he fell into a kind of trance, memorizing the pattern of the paint flaking off the HOTEL SACRAMENTO sign. It was time enough to grow impatient himself, to imagine that he *could* be brave when Dr. Chenoweth called him again.... But when Dr. Chenoweth did call, it seemed like no time at all. Back in the chair, John could fool himself for maybe thirty seconds that the drill didn't hurt as much as before. Then time, which had compressed itself into nothing, would stretch out so far that five minutes seemed like all afternoon....

"Your little sister doesn't make as much fuss as you do," his mother scolded him. "Dr. Chenoweth said you were about the *wiggliest* boy he'd ever seen."

But no matter how much he'd wiggled, or how miserable he'd looked, they hadn't let him go until the cavities were all drilled and silver was crimped into the holes in his teeth.

# # # #

And that was it, he thought now, pressing his back harder against the ground. Torture wasn't just being hurt. It was the way time stretched out; it was being helpless and naked. The Gestapo wouldn't even let him rest, the way Dr. Chenoweth had.

Voices echoed in his head:

Ve haf vays to make you talk....

Death is better than dishonor.

You aren't a crybaby, are you?

The Scout was dumb.

He felt the ants tickling; he thought of the Apaches staking people out over anthills. He tried to think of everything except how weak and slow his father had looked, climbing into the truck. He thought of snow – how an Indian kid his age might lie out there hunting, his skin tough because he'd never had to wear a shirt. Waiting for deer. He'd have to try it sometime, some winter. He shivered again....

But it was hard to think of snow in the drowsy warmth and pine scent of a July day. He pressed down still harder.

Ah. Finally. An edge of pain, like a thin, sharp rock digging into his right shoulder blade. He tensed himself, tried to be brave....

Then he heard a whoop.

Gary!

He looked out and glimpsed Gary and Jimmy coming up the street by Curly McPherson's house. No sign of Freddie. They had their guns drawn and were looking up toward the woods. He realized that they'd given up trying to find him; Gary had yelled to tell him where *they* were, if he was still in the war.

John felt suddenly guilty; the shock of it seemed to blend with the pain of the rock-edge under his back. *Jeez,* he thought. *I lost track of time. They must think I quit – ran out on them.* He straightened up to move, but as he did so, he automatically reached down to touch the rock – and stopped again as his fingers felt something he didn't dare believe.

An arrowhead?

Yes.

Half buried in the pine and fir needles, the blackened, rotted oak leaves and sticks.... The duff, his Cub Scout handbook called it. The duff of the forest floor.

The first one he'd ever found.

Awestruck, he held it in his hand and rubbed off the dirt: a chip of obsidian, black glass, from the great glass mountain out near Medicine Lake, where the Hillers had gone camping once with his father's Sacramento friends the Joneses. The Indians here must have traded for a lump of it. Then they'd heated it, maybe, to flake off smaller pieces, and finished it with bone tools. That's what his schoolbooks said. Then they'd shot it ... at a deer or a man?

Gary and Jimmy had disappeared behind his house.

John climbed out of the fort. The blood had drained from his head; branches whirled in the sun's glare. He slipped the arrowhead into his hip pocket and felt it there like a lucky charm, beating against him like a heart (or maybe it was his own blood beating). His fingers still felt the old, cold touch of the stone, the touch of the long-dead people who had made it, a breath of air like their voices. *They were real*, he thought. *They really lived here. Just like me....* And he thought (with only a little of that sense of watching himself, smiling at himself, that he'd had at the den meeting): *It's because I* was *brave that I found it. It's a sign, like an Indian boy would get.*

He moved north again, planning to circle down on the other side of Thelma Hoffman's house. Even up on the top of the bank he could smell it, hear the dogs barking inside.

Why doesn't she let them out? he wondered.

He came out above the corner of her house, at the edge of the woods. He drew the cap gun – after the arrowhead, it had never seemed so silly.

Time seemed to slow down ... but with excitement, not with pain. John looked north past the Sykeses' house, up the length of the canyon, and saw what he knew would be there (and felt a deep, quiet joy in knowing it, the way a compass needle always knew which way to point): the eastern half of Mt. Shasta, the bigger of its twin cones, more than fourteen thousand feet high. A dozen miles away, it stood out just as clear against the blue as the mountains close by. A single lens-shaped cloud hovered over the summit; its shadow darkened part of the slopes of gray volcanic rock, tinged with pink and purple. Only a few patches of white were left, in the hollows. One was a glacier; it curved around a ridge near the top like a question mark. What was it asking *him?* John wondered. The Indians, he knew, had worshipped the mountain. Their gods lived there.

At the same time he saw Mr. Sykes setting a box down in the dust of their yard. Their house, gray-brown shingles, looked as if it had never been painted; one end was propped up on posts against the slope, and John could see daylight under it. Mr. Sykes was showing his kids a bow-and-arrow set. He hadn't shaved; his T-shirt had holes in it. But he was laughing as he stood next to Jackpot and held the bow so that Jackpot could draw it with his good arm. The arrow flew over the box, into the woods. One of the younger kids – the boy – ran after it. *He shouldn't do that,* John thought. He almost yelled: *They might shoot again!* The arrow might be lost; it might have broken against a rock. It looked like a cheap set anyway, and John knew that the Sykes kids would break things even faster than he would.... But in spite of all this, he wished his own father were a little more like Mr. Sykes, who didn't seem to get mad, just stood there in the sun and scratched his head with a dirty hand. *Nobody's scared,* John thought. Though he knew his own father was better. *No excuse,* his mother had said about the Sykes kids' teeth. But John wasn't sure what was worse: having your teeth get all black and snaggly, like Jackpot's, or having to sit in Dr. Chenoweth's chair.

The Indians weren't scared, he thought. *They didn't have any dentists, either.*

The dogs in Thelma Hoffman's house barked louder, as if they could smell him outside.

Jackpot's second arrow hit the box, and the Sykes kids all cheered. Watching it flash, John felt exultantly that it was an answer to the mountain's question. He'd get his *own* bow and arrows....

He wanted to be an Indian.

Then Gary and Jimmy came around between the two houses, guns at the ready – the way Ronnie Knudson said he'd done in Korea.

John wanted to do it right. He crouched behind trees at the edge of the bank and waited until they were out in the open. "B'dam! B'dam!" he yelled, so that they'd know they'd been ambushed – that he *would* have killed them if this was for real. It was close enough range. *If I was them,* he thought. *I'd die. Even if it was Japs that shot me. After all, I deserve it. I was patient. I outflanked them....* But he knew they wouldn't think of it, and though the steady current of joy never stopped flowing through him, he felt a faint resentment as he dashed down the bank. He wasn't sure how the Japs charged – they yelled "Banzai!" or something, and waved swords – but he didn't have his sword, so he just ran zigzagging toward them like an infantryman, yelling, "B'dam! B'dam! B'dam!", even at top speed able to dodge the dog poop that littered the ground on Thelma Hoffman's side. (Bullets zipped past his cheeks; the wind was keen....) He ran almost up to Gary and Jimmy before he staggered, grabbed his side, twisted and fell in the dust.

"Gotcha," Jimmy said. "Dirty Jap."

John lay on his back, heart thumping. The warm dust against his skin felt soft as flour. He touched his pocket; the arrowhead was still there. (Jackpot's third arrow went *thunk* into the box.) The sun shone red through his eyelids; when he opened them, the sky was so high and blue that he almost wanted to cry.

There, he thought. *Now they've seen how* I *died, maybe they will too. And then it'll be* really *real....*

Jimmy poked him with his gun barrel, laughing. "You think we really killed him?"

"Don't know about them Japs," Gary said. "Maybe just playin' possum. Want to make sure?"

John thought they might kick him or something. He scrambled to his feet, and felt as dizzy as he had at the fort. "I found an Indian arrowhead up there," he said.

Gary squinted; he didn't seem to hear. "Where'd you go? We thought you'd quit."

"Up there," John waved vaguely. "I'm not gonna tell you where my hideouts are. You gotta find me."

"No fair just hidin'," Jimmy said. "It's supposed to be a war."

"If it was, I'd have got you. You'd be dead," John said. "I'm not kiddin'. I found an arrowhead. I'll show you.... Whcre's Freddie?"

"I don't know," Gary said.

"I left him behind to keep you guys busy."

"He must've gone home," Jimmy said.

"Never saw him," Gary said.

"I guess he didn't want to be a Jap," John said.

"Well, *somebody's* gotta be a Jap."

14.

The noon whistle blew.

His mother came out onto the porch. "John-*ny*!" she called.

"I'm coming!" he called back.

It was hot on the street. They looked for Thelma Hoffman on her porch, but she wasn't there. Sometimes she sat out in a rocker, with her swollen feet in fuzzy slippers up on the railing – seldom saying anything, just watching the kids play, sipping something that looked like iced tea.

"Whiskey," Gary had said once. "She drinks whiskey." But John wasn't sure. When his father drank whiskey, he used a little tiny glass, like the cowboys in the movies. A shot glass, he called it. Thelma Hoffman drank out of a tall glass with ice cubes in it.

John checked: his father hadn't come home. No truck. Just the sky-blue Chevrolet sedan his mother drove, parked in front of the retaining wall.

Gary was looking at it too. "Your pa like Chivies?" he asked. That was how he said it – the twang again.

"Yeah."

"My pa says a Chivy's good for speed, but you want it to last, you're better off with a Ford."

John didn't know what to say. He still didn't want to make Gary mad. Mr. Grissom worked in a garage, so he ought to know. But John thought *his* father ought to know what was a good car too.

"My dad *likes* 'em fast," he said.

His mother called down. "Hey! Lunch is ready."

"Do you want to eat lunch with us?" John asked suddenly. He wanted to change the subject ... and he still felt a little guilty about hiding from Gary and Jimmy all that time. Just looking for his father's truck had somehow taken the joy away; he couldn't imagine being an Indian now. "My mom won't mind."

"We'd better git on home," Jimmy said.

"She made biscuits this morning. And my mom makes the best biscuits in the world."

"What are you *doing* down there?" his mother asked.

"Can Jimmy and Gary eat with us?"

"I guess so." His mother's coppery hair was pinned back severely, except for one loose strand that fell over her forehead. She wore an apron; she leaned on the railing so that her elbows bent toward each other a little. "If it's OK with *their* mother."

"Gary," Jimmy said in a low, worried voice. "We're supposed to help Ma out. Remember?"

"It's OK," Gary said.

"No, it ain't. We'll git in trouble.... I ain't picked up them toys yet."

Gary was already climbing the steps. "We got plenty of time," he said. "But if you want to, go home. I don't care."

Jimmy paused at the bottom, eyes full of foreboding.

John clumped up past him. "Look!" he told his mother. "I found an Indian arrowhead."

"Really?" She started to smile. He dug for it in his pocket, but as he reached the porch he heard her gasp. The freckles on her face seemed to expand with indignation. "How come you have your shirt off? Didn't I tell you – " She pulled the wadded shirt from his belt; a cloud of dust puffed out and she sneezed. "What have you been *doing*? You're *filthy*, from head to toe." She held the shirt at arm's length by her thumb and forefinger and shook it, then dropped it to the floor. "Just filthy," she said. Cleo, who had been sleeping beside the door, lurched up, chain collar jingling, toenails clicking. His mother took John by the shoulders, the way Mrs. Ordoñez had, and turned him slowly around, swatting the dust from the back of his pants, while Gary grinned. "What were you playing – cowboys and Indians?"

"GIs and Japs," Gary said. "He was a Jap."

"Is that why he's so much dirtier than you are?" To John she said: "You know you have leaves in your hair? And *ants.*"

"I was up in the woods. That's where I found this," he said, holding out the arrowhead, almost in despair. How could he explain the joy of finding it – or how he'd *had* to flop full length in the dust if he wanted to die right?

"Lemme see that," Gary said, finally interested. John turned to him and Gary made a grab for it; then they were wrestling – strenuously but not quite seriously, because his mother was there. Gary's hot, sweaty arms had him in a hammerlock and were bending him down toward the floor when Cleo stiffened and growled.

Gary let go. "Hey, does she bite?"

"No, she's a good dog," John said, surprised. Still clutching the arrowhead in his right hand, he caught Cleo's collar with his left. He almost couldn't hang on, she pulled so hard, claws scraping on the boards. A low, tense rumble came from her throat.

"You shouldn't play around like that in front of her," his mother said. "She thinks Gary was really trying to hurt you."

"She *looks* like she bites," Gary said, edging away.

"I never saw her like this before," John said. "Honest. She never bit anybody." He was embarrassed for her, but also secretly glad to see Gary scared for once – to have Cleo try to protect *him*, even if he didn't need it. "Take it easy," he murmured, stroking the smooth top of her head. "Good dog. Good doggy."

"Well, whoever wants some lunch – " his mother said. "Where'd Jimmy go?"

"Home, I guess," Gary said. He sounded calm enough now, even scornful. "Jimmy's kinda shy."

No, he isn't, John thought, with a little of the same resentment he'd felt charging down the hill. His ears still throbbed where Gary's arms had squeezed them. He thought: *You shouldn't call Jimmy shy just because* you *got scared*. But that made him wonder. If Gary *could* get scared, then why wasn't he more afraid of his dad? Why hadn't he gone home, the way Jimmy had?

Connie Hiller looked concerned. "Well, he doesn't have to be shy around *us*. You're always welcome ... as long as your mother isn't expecting you or something."

"It's OK," Gary said.

"You sure? All right, then..... Whoever wants some lunch has to wash up *thoroughly* and put on some clean clothes." John knew she wasn't talking to Gary. "No, just leave that shirt right there. Don't bring it inside. I don't know why I even bother to do laundry."

# # # #

He laid the arrowhead on a bookshelf above his bed. (That was one reason the Hillers were different. Nobody in the neighborhood had so many books: shelved, piled and in boxes, in every room.) But first he'd sniffed it, put his ear close to it, hoping to hear again the faint whisper of those Indian voices. Nothing. Here it was just a rock. There were too many other whispers in the hot, airless house, too many smells, too delicate a balance between comfort and fear. In the bathroom, where he scrubbed himself, he saw the hairbrush his father spanked him with – yellow plastic against the white porcelain of the basin, stained with rust; a wet-pipe smell. And in his and Tommy's bedroom, where he put on clean jeans and a T-shirt, his father had torn out half a closet wall, leaving the bare studs. John could smell plaster dust, the heat of the power saw cutting (like the tooth dust and the heat of the drill in Dr. Chenoweth's office); he could hear the menace of the electricity crackling through the wire – and something else. He could feel the work itself, something heavy and dark in the air that made it hard for him to move or even breathe – the same way he'd felt trying to get the other

Cubs to make armor; something that told him: *You can't do this. Ever. It's hopeless even to try....* Next door, the dogs still barked.

15.

Annie and Clyde crossed the bare dirt past Dr. Malevich's house, near where the bulldozers were working on the freeway. There wasn't any shade. It was hot. Then they looked both ways to see that no cars were coming, and crossed Highway 99. They followed a little street down to the tracks. A freight train was just disappearing around a bend. They walked along the ties – big hunks of wood stained with black tarry stuff, sunk into the gravel. She stepped only on the wood, as if she were playing hopscotch. Even here it was hot. The sun burned down on her cowboy hat and her red-checked shoulders. She could see her shadow – short and fat; she kept stepping on it, as if it couldn't get out of the way. The tops of the rails shone. Big spikes nailed them to the ties. There was a hot, cindery metal smell. She and Johnny had put pennies on the rails once and let a train run over them to see what happened. They weren't supposed to do that, but they did. When the train had gone, the pennies were flattened and bright and the pictures on them were rubbed out. They weren't any good as money anymore, Johnny said.

"Here we go," Clyde said.

They were almost to the highway bridge. Clyde led her on a path down to the river. Annie scampered past him. It got cool, suddenly, and she could smell wet rocks and plants. A swarm of golden bugs no bigger than specks of dust swirled around her head. She sneezed and brushed them away. Then she came through to the river, and the concrete arches of the bridge far above, and the bridge's shadow. The river made a noise like people clapping, except it never stopped. It was all one noise, but she could hear the separate people in it, too. She looked back and saw Clyde still picking his way slowly down the path. "Hurry up!" she called. Clyde was old. But even when *she* was old, Annie promised herself, she wouldn't be slow.

Clyde gave her one of those rare smiles. "Got nothin' but time here."

Long green grass hung from some of the rocks like hair, swaying in the water. Annie saw willow trees and water plants with big leaves and stems, like rhubarb. She saw a wild blackberry bush, but the berries weren't ripe yet. Most were green, a few red. None black. She saw some kind of tree that, when the breeze off the river blew, the leaves flipped. over and turned from green to white, then green again. *How did that happen?*

Clyde had her sit on the biggest rock. It was gray and had scabby, mossy things on it. He baited her hook with a salmon egg. "No point in casting here," he said. "You'll just get your line snagged in all this stuff behind you. Just underhand it out there." She looked at him. "Just *toss* it, like a softball."

So she did. She let her feet hang down almost to the water, but not quite. It was nice and cool here. Under the water, the egg looked white instead of pink. It moved down with the current until the line was taut; then she pulled it back. Over and over. It was kind of like rowing, she thought. Meanwhile, Clyde put on his waders and walked out to where he had room to cast into riffles of white water. Annie was jealous of him. She wanted waders too. *How come I have to stay on this old rock?* Clyde moved knee-deep out into the sun, so that his hair shone white. She looked at the rutted back of his neck.

Soon Annie got used to the noise of the river, and could hear other sounds over it. She heard birds, and trucks roaring on the bridge, and sometimes a clocking sound as the current rolled rocks against one another on the bottom.

Time went by.

The noon whistle blew.

They took a rest and Annie ate her sandwich. Clyde drank coffee from a thermos and ate soda crackers. She drank river water from her cupped hands, so cold the roof of her mouth ached.

She felt disappointed, once again. Every time she'd gone fishing, she'd expected to catch a fish right away. Every time, she'd imagined it so clearly that it *had* to be true. Drop her line in. The fish – a big one, just waiting for her – would strike; her rod would bend; the reel would spin with a ratchety sound. Set the hook. Pull it out. But it never happened that way. Instead, she just sat on a rock until her tailbone was sore.

"Patience," Clyde told her. "That's the most important thing for a fisherman. Or woman. Patience."

"But where *are* the fish?"

"Oh, they're there. Lyin' low, this time of the day, but they're there. That's why I took you to this deep hole here. They're takin' a siesta down there, the fish, till it cools off in the evening and they come back up."

"Is this the wrong time of day?"

Annie had a first, faint suspicion then. Someday she would know that this wasn't *real* fishing – just something for little kids. But later still she would decide that Clyde had been as nice as he could be.

"Not necessarily," Clyde assured her. "Early morning and evening, that's good. But you'll get all the moskeeters out then. They'll bite you. You don't want that."

"No." Annie shuddered. "Skeeters!"

Another little smile. "Well, let's get at it, then."

Clyde gave her a new salmon egg. It was slippery and fishy-smelling. Annie had learned how to twist an egg onto a hook without tearing it apart or pricking herself. It wasn't easy, though. She dropped the egg into the dark green-brown pool and watched it get smaller and smaller as the current took it away.

Clyde waded out again. The water chuckled around his legs. Where he was, downstream from her, the river was bright and shallow and fast-moving, with gold and brown spots in it from the rocks underneath. Clyde was using one of the flies from his hat. Annie had watched her father tie flies. He had a little vise that screwed onto the edge of a card table and held the hook; then he'd wind colored thread on it. That was supposed to be a bug's body. And the thread held the feathers that were supposed to be wings. The flies had names, her father had told her. *Nymph. Royal Coachman. Gray hackle red. Or red hackle gray.*

Annie hummed the names. What kind did Clyde have?

Then, looking past him, she saw, far away, on the road on the other side of the river, her father's maroon pickup truck. And her father, standing beside it.

# # # #

Annie did remember the day when he had cracked her and Johnny's heads together. But she remembered it only as a vague dark spot, like the spot she'd see after she squinted into the sun and closed her eyes. She remembered being whipped – the stinging and burning of the willow switch on her legs. But she didn't think about either now. She was glad he was watching her, and proud. *See? I'm fishing!* She stood up on the rock so he could see her better. She straightened her back. She could see the shadow of her cowboy hat on the water.

Then something jerked.

"Hold on there!" Clyde shouted, splashing toward her.

Annie whooped.

16.

The house had seemed empty minutes ago. Now it was packed. Connie Hiller had to get Johnny cleaned up and into fresh clothes; she had to calm the dog, who had growled at Gary Grissom, nearly bitten him, maybe; she had to corral Tommy, who was caught up in all the excitement and was running from room to room, shouting. Now she had to set an extra plate for lunch. She took the fourth plate down from the cupboard again. Then she set out the sandwiches and soup bowls and glasses of milk. Johnny wanted to eat biscuits, too. He'd been bragging about them to Gary, apparently. So Connie set a plate of *them* out, though only a few were left over from breakfast – misshapen ones she'd baked from the last scraps of dough.

"Of course they're cold now," she told Gary. "I could warm them up – but that just makes them harder, I think."

"That's OK, ma'am," he said. Gary fascinated her a little. She hadn't seen him so close up before. The same age as Johnny, the same size, but altogether different – tanned and gritty-looking and somehow *adult*, with those strange pale eyes: a little man in a boy's body. And he had those Southern manners. "They sure taste good."

"I'm sorry it's just tuna sandwiches. We weren't expecting company."

"That's OK, ma'am."

He could have washed *his* hands, Connie thought, but it was good to worry about something besides Frank. She thought of Annie. Had a single sandwich been enough? If Clyde had so many pockets, maybe she should have given her more. She would fix a snack, maybe, when Annie came home. Tommy sat in his high chair, tomato soup staining his bib, milk on his chin, a smear of banana on one cheek. The two older boys were wolfing their food down, and Connie felt a twinge of envy: It would be years before *they* had to worry about their weight. Even Frank hadn't gained much yet ... but wasn't that the point: *not* to think about Frank?

"It sure tastes good, ma'am," Gary said. "You sure are a good cook."

"This isn't cooking. This is just opening a can and slicing some bread." Connie smiled. "But I'll tell you what, Gary. It makes a cook feel good, when she sees you men cleaning up your plates."

Men. The word hung in the air. Johnny shot her a pained look, and Connie understood it instantly. Once in a while this happened between her and Johnny – they were alike, in a way. She had never called *him* a man, not by himself – so just like that, he was wondering if she liked Gary better. So silly! The things Johnny let himself stew about! Sometimes she wished she could shake the silliness out of him. But she understood.

"You were playing war?" she asked.

"GIs and Japs," Gary said. "My pa fought the Japs."

"He did?"

"He was on Iwo Jima island. There was *big* fightin' there, he said. The Japs were hidin' in caves, and our guys had to go in after 'em with flamethrowers. It was the only way, Pa said. They wouldn't surrender, even when we had 'em beat."

"War can be terrible," Connie murmured.

"They started it. The Japs did."

She remembered. Her last winter in Oakland, her last as a single girl. When the news of Pearl Harbor came over the radio, she'd driven down to the shore of the bay, not knowing why, and stared across the grim gray water at the Golden Gate, though which the Japanese fleet might come steaming any moment. She saw the whitecaps blown up by the wind; even inside the car she was chilled. What she felt wasn't fear, exactly, but an emptiness, a void. *Everything's going to change, but into what? Nothing about life is ever going to be the same.* And she felt that way now. What was Frank...?

"Still," she said, "we did terrible things too. Like the atomic bomb. All those women and children who didn't – "

"My pa says," Gary said firmly, and Connie was startled to find that this little boy was *arguing* with her, in a grown-up way, as Johnny never could. "My pa says the A-bomb was a blessing from the Lord. They'd've had to land in Japan. Him and his buddies. My pa was all ready for it, he says. Him and all his buddies who were gonna get killed. My pa says he went right down on his knees there in Okinawa, where they were gettin' ready, and thanked God for the A-bomb. Because it saved more lives than it took. That's what my pa says. It was a sign."

"Does he talk about this often?" she asked.

"No, ma'am. He don't talk about it much at all. The war. But when he does, we sure listen."

I bet you do, Connie thought. That explained some of Gary's odd maturity: He was parroting the words of adults.

At that moment Tommy distracted her. Red soup drooling from his mouth, he began banging on the arm of the high chair with his spoon. He was talking to himself again, and pressing his hand against his mouth. "Yay, Tommy," she heard him say.

"Be quiet," Johnny hissed at him.

Connie understood this, too. He was embarrassed by Tommy, just as she was, no matter how hard she tried to fight it,

"What's wrong with him?" Gary asked.

"Nothing's wrong with him." Connie included Johnny in her glance: *Don't you dare.* "He's just fine."

Everyone shut up for a moment. Even Tommy.

"I just meant to say," she said, "that I guess we *had* to fight, but war's so terrible, even when it's just play.... I hope neither of you ever has to go for real."

That should have ended it, she thought. But Gary, like a little bull terrier, wouldn't let go. And right then Connie decided that she didn't like the boy. It was unfair, of course. She had too much on her mind today. He was only a child. But still....

"It's because we've sinned," he said solemnly.

"What?"

"We've let Satan loose. We gave him the power to make war because we listened to him. That's what Pastor Johnson says."

"Well, maybe so."

"It's the truth, ma'am. You ought to come to our church."

"We have our own church, Gary," Connie said – though that was stretching it. She had been raised as a Congregationalist, but there was no such church in Dunsmuir, so she went to the Episcopal services. Frank never attended church, though he said he believed in God. He insisted that organized religion was a con game; ministers were liars and frauds. (Again, why so *angry*?) "But thank you just the same."

"Are you saved?"

Gary's face flushed in spite of his tan. Connie thought: No, she didn't like him, but she had to admire him, somehow.

"Don't you think that's our business?"

"No, ma'am. It don't make any difference what church you go to if you ain't saved. That's just Satan talkin' – tryin' to deceive you." Gary swallowed; his Adam's apple pumped. "Besides, some of them other churches are just the Devil's work anyway. Pastor Johnson says they don't believe in the Bible anymore. All this evolution, how we come from monkeys...."

Connie knew Harold Johnson. She had taught his younger sister, Alice, her first year at the high school. She saw him now and then downtown, at the S&J or the bank. A pursy little man, she'd always thought, with a doughy, jowly face and a string tie. Pleasant enough. But how remarkable that this boy should invest him with the authority of an Old Testament prophet.

A thunderer.

"Pastor Johnson says all this schoolin' don't mean anything if you don't have faith. Like *him*," Gary said, pointing at Tommy – and now she knew he'd gone too far. "If you come to our church, Pastor Johnson could lay hands on him and heal him, even if the doctors can't. I seen him do it, lots of times."

"He isn't sick," Connie snapped. "Whatever gave you the idea he was?"

"I thought – "

"Well, he isn't. There's nothing wrong with Tommy."

And she glared down at Gary, hands on hips, until he lowered his eyes and fidgeted. *Darn* you, she thought, while Tommy, her sweet boy, seemed oblivious to it all, whispering to himself and banging the spoon.

Then Connie was sorry. Gary *was* just a child, and a guest. She was breathing hard; the sweat under her dress had gathered to beads, trickled down her sides.

She remembered one of her stepmother's maxims: *Horses sweat. Men perspire. Women glow.*

Well, she was glowing now, for sure.

"Gary, tell me," she said more gently. "This idea of inviting us to your church ... was that your parents' idea?"

"They talked about it," Gary mumbled, his face even redder.

"But you just decided to ask, right now?"

"Yes, ma'am."

"Well, tell them we appreciate it ... their concern. But you can't force things like this. If we ever *do* go, it'll have to be when we're ready. Not before."

# # # #

Later, washing the dishes, she asked Johnny: "Have you been talking about Tommy? To the other kids?"

"No."

"You must have said *something*. Or Annie. But probably you, if Gary knew."

"You said ... it was OK if we talked about him."

"I said you shouldn't be ashamed. It's not his fault he got so sick when he was just a baby. Three days old.... I guess there's no way to keep it a secret. It *isn't* a secret. But I wish you wouldn't...." Connie raised her hands out of the water and held them there, uncertain of what to say next. She wore rubber gloves; soap bubbles sleeved her freckled arms to the elbow. Detergent was hard on her skin. Like the sun. That was why she wanted Johnny to wear a shirt. *We aren't the kind of people who tan. We burn.*

"Mom, what did Dad do in the war?"

Connie knew he was changing the subject, but let it go. "Why do you want to know?"

"Well, Gary ... he was talkin' about *his* dad."

"He worked on the railroad," she said. "Right here in Dunsmuir."

"I mean in the Army. Wasn't he in the Army?"

She lowered her hands, peeled off the gloves and reached for a towel. "They wouldn't let him. They needed trained railroaders for the troop trains, all the freight they were sending up and down the coast. They'd call him up for the draft and the SP would get him deferred, every six months. Then they'd call him up again. It nearly drove him crazy."

"Oh," Johnny said, clearly disappointed.

And maybe Frank should have gone, Connie thought now. *He's always felt he missed something. A man's thing. A chance to prove himself, to see the world. An adventure.* But she remembered how she had felt at the time: *We just had a baby! We're just starting out! Why do you want to leave us and maybe get yourself killed, when you don't have to?*

"He wanted to go," she told Johnny. "Or at least he wanted to end the suspense. It was driving us *all* crazy. Finally he went and volunteered – didn't wait for the draft. But the Army didn't want him so much after all. He was twenty-seven, twenty-eight then. He was a father. They wanted young, single men more.... And the railroad still managed to hang onto him."

"Oh," Johnny said again.

The towel squeaked as she dried the glasses.

"If he *had* gone, he might not be here. Or Annie or Tommy either. Ever think of that?" She smiled. "I'm sure he was doing just as important a job here as Gary's dad. Or anyone. Then, the year before you arrived, when I went back home to Oakland when your Uncle George was sick, your dad worked baggage on the Oakland Pier, where all the soldiers were coming and going. They'd throw these big duffel bags at him – a hundred pounds, *two* hundred, some of them weighed – and he'd catch them and turn, like this, and stack them in the baggage cars." She was stacking the dishes in the cupboard. "If you ever wondered how your dad got so strong, that's one reason. But all that twisting ... it didn't do his back any good."

The same poor back that boxcar hit.

She turned back to Johnny, and he was still so droopy-faced that she said: "Don't look so *serious*. Not everybody gets to be a hero.... Why don't you show me that arrowhead you found?"

17.

Maybe he'd known earlier, Frank Hiller thought, Even as far back as when he'd hung up on the Trainmaster instead of saying something. Something he couldn't take back.

Maybe he'd known when he picked this stupid shirt out of the closet.

Or thought he saw Jamison at the crew dispatcher.

All the time, he realized now, even when he was crazy, he'd been protecting himself. Leaving himself a way out.

Frank wrestled with this idea. He stood and smoked and watched Annie and Clyde Carter stop fishing and eat, then pick up their rods again.

The lump in his gut wasn't squirming anymore with terror and hope. It just sat there, heavier and bitterer every minute. Like a rock. He had let the old man down, and his grandpa too. His moment had come, and already it was gone. He was on his knees, beaten like them – only worse; it seemed that he'd hardly fought. And right then, Frank began the long task of persuading himself that he *hadn't* chickened out, just grown up. He'd put his family first, not run off from his responsibilities like some asshole. That's why he'd hedged his bets all along. Frank would come to believe this, but it wouldn't be easy for him, or quick.

It would be like busting up that granite boulder jammed against the back porch with nothing more in his hands than a crowbar. Knocking off little chips of it. Dust.

The boulder was inside him now. The bruise was part of it, part of the same pain.

He still blamed Connie for letting *him* down.

She *cared*, he'd thought as he lay in bed and she poured the lotion over him.

But it wasn't the kind of caring that did him any good.

The kids, maybe. But not him.

And he still cursed the SP and Ross. They had no right, he thought. No right to do this to him. *They* were the assholes.

All Frank could do now was knock off the first chip. He remembered taking her brother, George, barely recovered from his illness, still hobbling on a cane, his knuckles white, to this same stretch of river. George didn't have to climb much here. He could almost stand on the road and cast.

Frank had been wrong about that. Her family *had* had some hard times.

He watched Annie.

And it would seem to him, after enough of the boulder had been chipped away, that she was the main reason he'd stayed. How could he leave his little girl? He'd said something to Annie when he stormed out of the house. Something mean. He couldn't remember – but he was sorry for it now.

Frank admired how Annie never looked at him. Not once. She was concentrating, by God. Fishing for all she was worth. Good for her. After a while he tried to beam his thoughts in her direction – tried to get her to turn, to wave. That usually worked. And maybe she did see him finally. He thought so. But she wouldn't admit it, even then. *Damn.* She'd been sitting on a big rock; now she stood up. Her back straight. Her line, invisible until then, catching the sun.

Frank smiled.

Yes, that's what caught him, he would think in years to come. That wisp of iridescence in the air, binding him to her, as strong as spider's web.

Monofilament.

18.

"Isn't it beautiful?" his mother said. "People used to find them all the time, they tell me, but not so often these days. You should take it to school and make a report on it."

But the arrowhead was still just a rock. In John's bedroom the hot sunlight through the yellow-brown windowshade made the air seem heavy, as if he were under water. The room still had its vague menace. He felt guilty – for what, he wasn't sure. Getting so dirty? Inviting Gary for lunch? Wishing his father had been a soldier? *Something.* He had to do something. He shoved his head up under her arm, pressed it to her side and hugged her around the waist. He closed his eyes; she smelled of detergent and perfume and a warm, familiar smell – herself.

He remembered the argument that morning.

"I love you, Mom," he said.

"Well, I love you too," she said, startled, and hugged him back. He opened his eyes; it was all right.

# # # #

Where I grew up, he would tell somebody, sometime, *bears used to come down out of the woods, right to our house, before the freeway got built.*

They were black bears. John had never seen them – only heard them a couple of times, at night, like the boulder crashing down. But Cleo could smell them – a smell like an invisible current of terror that raised the hairs on her back like electricity. The only other thing that scared her so much was a thunderstorm.

Now he and the dog lay side by side again on the back porch, in the long peace of a summer afternoon, and the only smells were of pine lumber, dog poop, of course, Cleo's own smell and the scent of the trees above the bank, which sweetened the outdoor air even on the hottest days – which, like his fear, grew fainter and fainter but never entirely disappeared. He wore the cap gun again – "You'd wear that thing to school if I didn't make you take it off," his mother had said – but he was thinking about how to get that bow-and-arrow set. Sell Christmas cards door to door? He'd seen an ad for that in Boys Life. A recurved fiberglass bow, Port Orford cedar arrows.... It sounded like an awful lot of trouble, though. The dog whimpered in her sleep; her hind feet twitched.

"Chasing rabbits," he said. That was what everybody said when a dog dreamed, but as far as John knew, Cleo had never chased a rabbit. Only ducks and geese and quail and pheasants. She was half Irish setter and half Chesapeake Bay retriever, with curly hair on her body and smooth flaps for ears. A bird dog. Her ribs rose and fell; her muzzle lay flat on the boards. Her nose was black. He remembered how, two weeks ago, she was sleeping just like this on the living-room floor and he'd tried to throw darts as close to her nose as possible without hitting it, like a knife-thrower in a circus. The first one stuck three inches away. The second one ... just flopped on the carpet, but a dark-red drop of blood suddenly shone on her nose. And her eyes opened wide. He still felt sick inside to think about it. Her eyes hadn't looked hurt or accusing at all – just surprised. Which made it even worse.

Now Cleo stretched – she'd heard his voice – and those brown eyes opened again. Still nothing. No sign that he'd hurt her; no sign that she even remembered – except in her dream, and that was the bears, more likely. Maybe he was the only one who remembered now. She hadn't been able to tell anyone – wouldn't have, probably, even if she could.

Her tail thumped. She loved him. (Look at how she'd growled at Gary!) And he loved her....

But if he loved her, how could he have done it?

We've sinned, Gary had said.

That was true. John knew he had.... But did that mean he had to join Gary's church?

"Hey," he whispered and petted her, stroked her all along her side, but his new uneasiness wouldn't go away. He was trying to tell her with his touch that he wouldn't ever hurt her again. But that meant reminding her that he *had* hurt her. It wasn't that he was afraid she wouldn't trust him anymore. She would. That was the difference between dogs and people. But he wouldn't be able to trust himself. No matter how gently he touched her now, he would always feel himself holding back from what he *could* do. Had done. In some strange way, being nice to her was just the other side of torturing her. Not something different. Because he knew ... that although her teeth were sharp, her jaws strong enough to splinter the bones in his arm, she was helpless. Because she loved him. The way only an animal could.

"Good dog," he said.

Still, he knew, Cleo loved his father more. Frank Hiller didn't spend hours fussing over her, the way John did; he just gave her an occasional word or a pat on the head. But he took her hunting. He was proud of Cleo, and let her know it – proud of how this half-breed bitch, runt of the litter, that he'd picked up free from another railroader down in Gerber could outhunt his friend Bob Chapman's hundred-dollar pure-bred Irish. How without any training at all, just by instinct, she knew how to work up slowly on quail so they wouldn't flush with the hunters still out of range. "That big red goes lollopin' in there like a race horse – I thought Bob would have a heart attack, yellin'." How one bitter morning at Tulelake she'd swum through a knife-edge of ice that cut her legs to retrieve a Canada goose that turned out to be only winged. "You know how big a honker is. She can hardly get her jaws around him, and he's whalin' away at her, right in the face, with the other wing. But she brought him in. She has guts."

John would hear the pride in his father's voice, and for a moment Cleo's glory would warm him too. "Good dog," he'd tell her when she came back from the field – muddy and footsore, with ticks on her, exhausted and triumphant. But the thing was, she seemed to know she was good, beyond any praise John could give her. Her pride belonged to the men's world, closed off to him. He would have to become a hunter too. (When he got a real gun....) Because what Cleo loved best, John knew, wasn't his own kind of shamefaced gentleness, but his father taking out his shotgun to clean it: unzipping the case and putting oil on round white cloth patches and ramming them down the gleaming barrels. An instant before, she might have been asleep, dead to the world, sprawled and snoring by the stove, but the sight of that gun would electrify her – like the smell of the bears, only this time with joy: like what John had felt finding the arrowhead, but even greater, he thought: more joy than any person could feel.

And it really was his father she loved, John knew, not just the hunting. *He* wouldn't throw any darts at her, at least.

19.

Annie nearly fell off the rock. She'd hooked a trout without even trying. The rod creaked and the reel whirred and the fish danced on top of the water. She pulled, and the fish pulled back. She could feel its silvery strength pumping up through the line. She was scared it would break loose. But Annie was stronger. She jumped down to the shore, hanging onto the rod, and pulled again, and suddenly there it was, flopping in the shallows at her feet. She dropped the rod (without realizing it) and scooped the fish up with her hands and threw it onto the land. It was slimy and shockingly alive. Clyde came in beside her as she chased it over gravel and little pools and clumps of grass. It had lost the hook – free. She was shrieking.

"It's getting away!"

"Now, hold on ... hold on."

The fish wiggled, impossible to catch, and she thought it would crawl into the bushes and escape. Or get back into the water. But then it slowed down.

Gasping.

She could hear Clyde's hoarse breathing in her ear.

It'll die, Annie thought suddenly. The wet fish, as it lay there on its side, with a leaf sticking to it, was beautiful. Dark black-speckled green on top, rainbow colors in the middle, a silvery white below. Its gills gaped red as it tried to breathe. Its mouth opened and closed. And she felt an unexpected, terrible sadness. Catching fish was one thing. But she'd never thought about having to kill them.

Put him back, she wanted to tell Clyde. *Please! Let him live. I don't care.*

But Clyde had gripped the trout in his big chapped hand. He whacked its head on a rock, once, twice. Then it lay still.

Annie felt sick, but Clyde was smiling at her.

"Your very first, by golly. A nice little rainbow there."

"Is it dead?" she asked.

"Sure thing. Better get hold of your rod there, before it floats downstream. And your hat, too."

"My hat?"

It had fallen off, and she ran to get it. Clyde picked up the fish, wrapped it in wet grass and put it into the creel. By then Annie felt better. She sun warmed her wet hands and feet. A dribble of water from the cowboy hat tickled her neck. She could feel a grin growing wider on her face, stretching out both her cheeks. *I did it!* She remembered her father then. *He saw me! He saw me catch a fish!*

But across the river, he and the truck had gone.

# # # #

Well before Clyde came clumping up the front steps, Annie had run back and told her mother.

Tommy, all excited, trotted up to look at the fish. He tried to pet it. He made noises as if *he* had caught it and people were cheering. Cleo – let inside again – sniffed at it, and sniffed at Annie too.

"How big is it? Can you measure?" she asked. So her mother went and got the ruler. The fish was just over seven inches long.

"Is that *all*?" Annie said. When she had fought it in the water, when it had flopped on the shore, it had seemed so much bigger.

"Good eatin' size," Clyde said. "What you call a pan-size trout."

"Can I eat it?" She turned to her mother. "Can you cook it for dinner?"

"I suppose so," Connie Hiller said. "But you'll have to clean it."

"Aw, Mom."

Clyde actually chuckled.

"That's what I used to tell her Uncle George. Anyone who catches a fish has to clean it.... Are you sure you don't want something? I can make some iced tea."

Clyde shook his head. "Martha'll have lunch." That was Mrs. Knudson, his sister.

"Well, all right, then." Annie had the funny feeling that her mother wanted Clyde to be gone. "But thanks again for taking her. You're a very patient man."

"No trouble," Clyde said. "No trouble." He took off his canvas hat and scratched his head. "She's a good fisherwoman. Better than her brother is, even though he's older. He lets his mind wander. Doesn't pay attention. But Annie here, she's got the stuff."

"Still," Connie Hiller said. *She's mad*, Annie thought. *But why? I caught a fish!* It seemed as if Clyde would stand there and talk forever, which was exactly what her mother didn't want.

"Now that she's caught one," Clyde was saying, "she'll be hooked for sure."

Tommy kept grabbing for the trout. Annie loved her little brother. He was sweet most of the time. He followed her around and hugged her. His gray eyes were so deep and clear. But now she pushed him away, and he fell. Cleo jingled and barked. Tommy cried.

It was horrible, when everybody should have been glad.

# # # #

In the kitchen, later, her mother showed her how to clean a fish. "Just this once," she said. "Then you're on your own." She was trying to be nice now, Annie could tell, but she was still mad about something. And not just Tommy.

Her mother laid the trout on a cutting board on the counter. It was dull now, with the grass picked off it, and almost dry, though it still felt heavy and cold. The green part looked almost black; the rainbow colors had faded. One eye – where Clyde had slapped it against the rock? – was torn loose.

The fish was really dead.

"See? You cut here," her mother said. "Straight up from this thing."

"What *is* that?"

"It's what a fish pee-pees with. Or poo-poos."

It looked like a belly button, Annie thought. A little circle thing with a pinhole in it.

"Does a fish poo-poo?" she asked.

"I *guess* so," her mother said. "I hadn't really thought about it, to tell you the truth. Fish eat things. Bugs. So I guess they'd *have* to, don't you think?"

Annie giggled.

Her mother took a knife and slit the fish's belly from the circle thing up to the gills. "Now comes the hard part," she said. She put down the knife and hooked her forefinger under the throat of the fish and pulled until something snapped. The sides of the fish's head – its cheeks? – fell apart. Then she reached into the opened belly and peeled out the fish's purple guts.

"Eeuw," Annie said.

"At least they come all in one piece. Trout aren't bad."

With her fingernail, her mother scraped black stuff off the fish's backbone. Then the inside of it was clean – pink-white, with rows of tiny ribs. Her mother ran water from the faucet through it. "OK," she said. "Then we put it in the fridge and that's it, till dinner."

"I don't know," Annie said.

She wasn't sure she could use that big, sharp knife. She might cut herself. But she also meant ... what was it?

The sun had moved west by now. Light slanted in through the back window. She felt a little of the sadness she'd felt on the riverbank. She could smell it. When she was sad in the future, Annie wouldn't remember the dying fish with the leaf stuck to it, or the dead fish on the counter with its torn-out eye, or Tommy's face when she'd pushed him, or her disappointment that nobody had cared as much about catching the fish as she had, or that slant of yellow light. But she would smell all these things at once, somehow.

"Don't let Johnny eat my fish," Annie said. "*I* caught it."

"Don't worry, dear. It isn't big enough to – "

"I *mean* it! It's *my* fish." She knew Johnny would be jealous of her. He hadn't caught any trout yet. And he was older.

"OK, OK," her mother said.

But her mind still seemed to be on something else.

Then Annie remembered what had happened that morning – how she'd heard angry voices right here in the kitchen, and come in, scared but curious, and there was her mother with her face flushed and her mouth pressed tight and her father with a big vein sticking out in his neck. They shut up when they saw her. But they still *looked* mad.

"I don't even know where your brother is," Connie Hiller said. "Out back, I think. Or at Hughie's. I wish I knew where your *father* is. That's the question."

"I saw Dad!"

"What? You did? While you were fishing?"

"Over there," Annie said, pointing vaguely in the direction where the maroon truck had been.

"What was he doing?"

"Watching me. He saw me catch it! I think he did. He was just standing there by the truck."

"Where did he go, then?"

Annie shrugged. In all the excitement when the trout hit her line, had she glimpsed the truck moving away on that road across the river, back toward the middle of town? Or was she making it up? She pointed again – south.

"You sure?"

"No," Annie said. She shook her head. "Maybe." She had hoped this news was what her mother had been waiting for. For a moment, it seemed to be. She hoped it would make her mother happy. But it didn't.

20.

Frank Hiller did drive south. He doubled back on the same road, which the river would wash out in a few years. Even now, between the point where he'd entered it and a point across the river from the roundhouse, it was only a single lane of crumbling asphalt and dusty potholes. Barely enough room for the truck's wheels. But he'd rather go this way than back downtown. He drove along Butterfly Avenue, with its old two-story frame houses where Dunsmuir's Negro families once had been forced to live, and most still did. Bright-colored laundry on lines. Junk cars. Kids. The street was on low ground; it often flooded in a wet winter. Then Frank headed down South First Street, with Girard Ridge on his left and the river on his right. Through the trees on the riverbank he could see the SP yards: lines of rust-red boxcars, switch engines, the web of rails. Long shimmering arms of steel. The Octopus, reaching out for him.

And the SP would have him, he knew. That was decided. But not quite yet.

Let 'em wait.

He stopped again where South First began to curve back west toward the highway. The street crossed the river and the tracks near where a creek came in, shallow in its bed of round white stones. Connie and the kids used to park there sometimes and wait when he went out on a South End Pool trip; he'd wave from the caboose; they'd wave back. He could see Castle Crags from here – gray spires and domes of granite south of Mt. Bradley, with sun and shadow tracing every line of them. Frank climbed out of the truck and stood. He winced. He spread his feet to lower himself a little – tried to get as comfortable as he could – and rested his elbows on the hood. The metal was hot. He smoked more cigarettes. *Might as well smoke 'em all.* Over the steady sound of the river, he listened to the chugging and banging from the yards – that whole SP world that, for an hour, had wavered and become unreal. Now it would have to be real again.

But not quite yet.

It seemed to Frank that this might be the last free afternoon of his life. Free even though in truth he was already caught, like the last few Apaches in a James Warner Bellah story he'd read in the Saturday Evening Post: riding, twisting, running out of food and water, slitting their horses' veins and drinking the blood, to elude the cavalry one last time. And just because he couldn't get away, he let himself imagine what it would be like if he could.

Just start up and go. I've got gas. The canyon had only two exits, north and south. He didn't know north so well. So he'd probably head south, back into the Sacramento Valley, all that yellow grass, where the sky and the earth expanded to their full width. Big puffy white clouds, air crawling with heat. He'd pass through Del Paso Heights. But when Frank thought about it, he knew damn sure that his mother would never approve of his leaving his family; and his father ... well, the old man had lung cancer – *from cigarettes just like these,* Frank thought grimly but with a certain defiance, too, watching the smoke curl up: *As if anybody cared* – and wasn't in any shape to deal with this. Only Ralph, he realized with some surprise, might be willing to hear him out. His brother the engineer, with his narrow lips and coldly logical mind. Ralph would listen quietly, nodding. As if everything Frank told him he'd already known a long time ago. *Even though Ralph hasn't done any living at all, himself.* Understanding but offering no comfort. Frank longed even for this, but then he thought: *Hell, no, I won't stop. I'll just keep moving.*

He remembered the trip to Tempe with Bud Jones; it seemed to him now that this was the happiest he'd ever been, though it hadn't seemed that way then. They'd been on their own, he thought. Two young bucks. Free. What could be better than that? In the mornings, when the desert air was briefly cool, they'd get out of the Model A and yawn and stretch and play catch by the side of the road. The spiny bushes throwing long shadows. The hills, all rocks, sharp in the early light. Birds. Lizards. The feel of their muscles unstiffening and the smack of the ball in their gloves, back and forth, the rhythm of it. The smell of the dirt. Ahead of them a cheap but good breakfast at some diner: bacon and eggs and hashed browns and toast and coffee. And then driving on.

All we needed was a little more money. Then we could have stayed around. Maybe changed that coach's mind.

But this time, Frank knew, he wouldn't stop in Tempe or anywhere else. He'd drive clear to Mexico. Find himself a job. Meet some pretty *señorita*, maybe.

He spent quite a while imagining this woman – what she would look like. Smaller than Connie. Slimmer, anyway. Long dark hair, dark eyes, dark nipples. A shy yet incandescent smile. Mostly he thought of her skin: how it would be brown and warm, almost hot; how it would never feel cold when he touched it, even in the winter – what winter they had in Mexico. A warm *señorita* to lie beside. That was enough. Who cared if she had an education? Who even cared if she spoke much English? She would be smart enough, Frank thought; he wouldn't be attracted to her if she wasn't. Maybe it would be better without so much talking. They would understand each other....

But the trouble with this line of thinking was, it kept going. Sooner or later, there would be more kids. *Lots* of kids; she'd be Catholic. Mouths to feed. He would have to go to work again – serious work, not just enough to keep them in tortillas and beer.

And then the trap would close again.

What could he do? Frank didn't know much Spanish. He supposed he could work at a gas station, but what would that pay? Damn little.

Mexico had railroads, of course, but he wasn't sure that the SP couldn't reach across the border and blacklist him even there, the way it had blacklisted Dyke in that novel. Who knew? Even if the SP couldn't, he thought, what would life be like as he and the woman and the kids grew older – him still a brakeman, working the same crazy hours for less money, fewer benefits, no insurance if he got hurt again?

He was thirty-eight already.

Frank remembered what his grandpa had said: *That's what the sonsabitches want. To turn us all into Mexicans. Stoop labor.*

He'd be doing that to himself.

21.

What energy the ordinary kid had! John would think.

Later that afternoon he took a pick and a shovel from the porch and started digging in the bank behind the house.

He wanted to dig a hideout. An underground room, like some kids had built in a book he'd read. Only they'd dug it in a flat meadow and put the sod back on it for a roof. His plan was to dig straight in from the bank, maybe twenty feet, and run an escape tunnel up to the woods.

The thing about books, though, was that they never told you how hard it was. The surface of the clay was dry and cracked. When he broke through that with the pick, he got darker and redder; a couple of feet in, it was damp enough to stick to the shovel. In the winter, springs oozed out of every square yard of the hillside; the clay slid.... He dug out rocks, chopped through the fringe of tree roots that hung down from the top of the bank. He got tired. Still, it felt good sweating in the sun. Inside, the tunnel was nice and cool. A good place to hide. If he made some kind of a door – a flap of canvas, maybe – he could curl up in there, like a hibernating bear. Nobody could bother him. Maybe then he could have visions, like an Indian. At least get rid of that sick feeling in his stomach....

Clean living?

He wondered what that was. He'd read about it in a Hopalong Cassidy comic book. Hoppy rode into a town where people kept disappearing, and a man named Hiram Fleer, who owned a wax museum, made statues of them, one by one, and charged money to see them. John remembered his name because it reminded him of Fleer's bubble gum. Of course, it turned out that Hiram Fleer had killed those people; he'd soaked their bodies in a huge tank of molten wax and stood them up stiff so that the visitors to his museum *thought* they were statues. Hoppy found out when he sneaked into the museum at night and held up a candle to one of their faces; the wax melted right off. Then Hiram Fleer jumped on Hoppy and almost shoved him into the boiling tank. Hoppy was an old guy; his hair was white. But *a lifetime of clean living* – that's what it said – gave him the strength to slip Fleer's hold and throw him into the tank instead.

Just like magic.

John figured it probably just meant not smoking cigarettes or drinking whiskey. Stuff like that. But maybe it meant something more. Like Gary's church. Or like an Indian purifying himself so that he could stand pain. Or like his father, knowing he didn't have to pet Cleo all the time to make her love him....

"Hey there, prospector," his mother said.

She was looking up at him, a basket of laundry on her left hip, shading her eyes with her right hand. The sun was in the trees now; the shadow of the bank reached almost to her feet.

"Come down here a minute. What are you digging for?"

He told her.

"I don't know." She bit her lip. "I'm worried it might slide down on you when you're in there. You'd be buried alive."

"It won't cave in," he said, remembering the book.

She shook her head. "It might. I don't think you ought to take that chance."

"Aw, Mom."

"I'm sorry," she said. "You've done all that work. I didn't know what it was, or I'd have stopped you earlier. You were just working away like a little beaver – almost two hours, did you know that? Why can't you put that much energy into something useful? Here, you can help me with the laundry."

"Aw, Mom." *That wasn't work*, he wanted to say. *That was fun*. But if she thought it was work.... "I've already got it in so far. I can't quit now."

"Yes, you can. Come on."

He threw down the pick, too hard, and she gave him a look that meant business.

"And put that away.... You're all *dirty* again! I just washed your other ones. The least you can do is help me hang them up."

It was true. He'd tried to be careful, but, climbing down into the sunlight, John saw that his arms and pants legs were smeared stiff with clay. There was grit in his hair and down his neck.

"I could just cry," his mother said. "I know you aren't looking forward to when school starts, but I am.... Don't touch them. Just hand me the clothespins."

The clotheslines stretched parallel to the house and the bank, from the porch to a post near Thelma Hoffman's house. Following his mother as she hung the clothes, John looked down at the bleached dirt, pebbles, footprints, and felt hypnotized, all the energy draining out of him. His arms ached. He seemed to plod in slow motion. When they reached the far end, he heard Mrs. Hoffman's dogs yap louder, heard the whining of cats. Even Cleo, who had ignored them, came jingling over to sniff.

"Why doesn't she let 'em out?" John asked.

"Maybe there's something wrong," his mother said.

The sun slanted on the gray, peeling boards of Thelma Hoffman's house, rotten where they touched the ground. The smell of dog poop was powerful here. "Are you *sure* I can't dig a hideout?" he asked.

"*Yes*, I'm sure."

Then Annie came out on the porch. She waved and yelled. "Johnny, I caught a fish! You wanna see my fish?"

They turned. The basket was empty now. "That's right," his mother said. "Your sister caught a nice trout."

"Well, *I* found an Indian arrowhead," John yelled back at Annie, but he knew that didn't sound nearly as good as a fish. "I bet Clyde caught it," he said, climbing the steps. "He just let you *pretend* it's yours."

"Did not!" Annie said.

"Clyde said she caught it," his mother said, "and I believe him."

"It's *my* fish!"

John knew she was telling the truth. He just didn't want to admit it, after all his work on the hideout had been wasted. How come Annie was so good at things? Baseball. Fishing. She was a girl, wasn't she?

Now he had to go inside and look while his mother opened the refrigerator and Annie showed him the fish on a plate.

"Aw, that's just a little one," he said. "No bigger'n a bullhead."

"Is not!" Annie said, and she looked ready to cry – or fight. "Don't you try to eat it, either."

"Is too!"

"That's *enough*," his mother said – so sternly that it would have surprised John if she hadn't been in such a bad mood all day long. "Both of you. I can't take any more of this. Quarreling. Just get out of here for a while. Go play over at Hughie's or something. I don't care."

22.

Tommy needed his nap – all of a sudden, after so much excitement. Connie Hiller laid him on her and Frank's double bed, on a small rubber sheet. He still wet the bed more often than not. She lay down beside him, watching him sleep. Were Tommy's eyes *too* deep-set, she wondered for the thousandth time, were his lips *too* loose as he breathed in and out so peacefully, or did he look like any other four-year-old? Connie never could be sure. She laid a hand on his forehead. Warm but not feverish. Tommy grunted without waking up. *What kind of dreams does he have?* she found herself wondering. *Just like ours, or something strange and wonderful?* She edged away and stretched out on her back, on top of the bedspread, her arms and legs wide, so that no two parts of herself touched. Even holding herself still, she was sweating again. The house was at its hottest now, in late afternoon, when the outside air was already beginning to cool. Connie could smell herself; she could smell Frank – the lotion she'd put on him – even with the sheets changed.

Before long she felt itchy and drowsy. Her head ached.

Alone with Tommy in the morning, she had longed for somebody to talk to – though she probably wouldn't have talked about Frank. At lunch, surrounded by chattering kids, she had felt even more alone. Now as she stared up at the unfinished ceiling – bare beams and wires, spider webs and pads of insulation – Connie felt herself sinking into a despair she'd known only once before.

That was four years ago, after Tommy had been born, gotten so horribly sick and recovered – only days, really, since she'd floated into the depths of a benign universe and thought: *Why do we struggle? It's all so simple.* So much had changed – and so quickly, before the smell of that forest fire up by Black Butte had even blown away. It hadn't been so bad, Connie thought, when there was still a chance Tommy might die; fear had aroused her then to a desperate struggle. It was only when the danger was over and she and this pale, quiet baby, shrunken to half his birth weight, were back on Shasta Avenue that she lost all her strength. She lay on her bed, just as she was lying now. Her limbs heavy, unwilling to move. The very sunlight through the window somehow darker. Connie had heard of postpartum depression, but she'd experienced none of it with her first two babies. In fact, she hadn't ever quite believed in it, as a legitimate complaint. It made no sense. Only an unnatural mother, she had always thought, wouldn't be delighted with a newborn. But that fall, even when Connie forced herself to get up and care for Tommy, she moved around the house in a stupor. The railroad was busy then; Frank was seldom home. She couldn't keep up with the cooking and scrubbing and ironing. The other children roamed wild. So her stepmother came. Connie would have preferred Henrietta, but *she* was pregnant again. Anybody but her stepmother – though, to be fair, Nellie Ames Weldon had turned out to be a good grandmother for Annie and Johnny. More relaxed, more fun-loving than in Connie's own childhood, so that the kids enjoyed her nervous sparkle. If she *had* changed – and Connie hadn't spent more than holidays with her for several years now – what was there to fear?

She soon found out. Her stepmother came with the fall rains – in Dunsmuir, sometimes, it could rain for a solid month. Clouds hung deep in the canyon; the leaves fell; the black branches of the oaks dripped. The light was gray. Her stepmother looked the house over, and everywhere she looked, it changed. Connie felt like a child again, seeing everything through the older woman's eyes. The peeling paint, the muddy back yard. Threadbare carpets, unwashed linen, dishes in the sink. The *squalor* of the place, like some hovel in darkest Appalachia. *Tobacco Road.* Connie didn't have the energy to argue that it hadn't always been such a mess – and that Frank had plans to fix it up. Instead, her stepmother made *her* believe it was hopeless, as anyone would have known who wasn't foolish enough to go and live in the middle of nowhere with a railroad man who was gone most of the time.

Not that her stepmother blamed Frank. *He* was working hard enough. She blamed Connie for lying down on the job. "You think it was easy when I married your father and came into a house with two girls I didn't even know? I had no experience with babies or children at *all*, but I was expected to take charge. And I did. You think that was easy? *Nothing* about life is easy. I thought you'd learned that already. A woman's life, anyway. Now this baby, he *needs* you, and why you think you can take time off now, after what *he's* been through, I can't for the life of me...."

Chin up.

As far as Connie knew, Nellie Ames Weldon had never needed more than six hours' sleep in her life. She had never been depressed. She took charge again, mouth pursed with disapproval. She spat orders. Her skinny arms and legs – her right wrist had a wen on it the size of a robin's egg, which fascinated the children – were a blur of action. The dog slunk away. In next to no time, she'd whipped 305 Shasta Avenue back into shape. When she left after five weeks, Connie thanked her, weeping. But not from gratitude. No. Those were tears of humiliation. Connie hadn't grown up after all. She was still thirteen: too clumsy and too big (the tallest in her eighth-grade class, boy *or* girl; she'd never forgotten that), too careless and absent-minded, and worst of all (she'd always suspected) too blatantly ... well endowed. All the nights her stepmother was in Dunsmuir, Connie had gritted her teeth and curled up in bed, trying to shrink herself. She'd pulled the blanket up over her breasts, full and sore, and the rest of her, still flabby from Tommy's birth. She was still an oversized child, drying supper dishes in the kitchen in Oakland. Nothing in between had ever happened. When her stepmother found cold dishwater in the tablespoons next morning, she made Connie and Henrietta drink it. *It won't kill you. But it'll make you remember.* Connie remembered, all right. The awful taste. The shame. The ingenious cruelty of it – if they complained (and they never did), people would only laugh.

Had her father known?

Surely not. But what if he had?

Connie would never think ill of her father, and she didn't now. He was the soul of kindness. He always would be. But just for this moment, lying beside Tommy, worrying about Frank, she wondered if, just maybe, that kindness had its limitations. If, in regard to her stepmother, it hadn't been a form of ... weakness?

Would he have stood up to her, condemned her? Connie couldn't imagine it.

That's just lovely, Nellie.

And she felt a faint stirring of rebellion, which she promptly quashed. For if her father had been weak – which she wouldn't admit longer than it took to say the word – so was she. Had she ever stood up to Frank when *he* disciplined the kids?

No. Not even when he whipped Annie with that switch.

Frank was horrified afterward. Those welts! "My God, I didn't mean to ... I didn't think I'd hit her so hard," he'd confessed to Connie, on the point of tears himself. No, he wasn't a cruel man. She'd been sure of that when she married him.

And wasn't it best if parents agreed – if they kept a united front?

That's what she always told herself. Some spanked their children – that's how Frank had been raised – and some didn't. Did it really make all that much difference?

No, Connie would think when this day was over, and for most of the days to come. *It doesn't. Not really. We've done the best we can. The kids are fine.*

But at this moment, when even thoughts of her father failed to bring her the usual comfort, a new and disturbing idea occurred to her: of a *chain* of weakness. Her stepmother had diminished her while her father looked away. Then she had looked away while Frank did what *he* wanted. For there was never any question of whose system of punishment would prevail. He had always seemed so ... certain.

I'm not supposed to be their buddy. I'm supposed to be their dad.

Once she'd told him, about Johnny: "That boy's afraid of you. Afraid of his own father. I don't know why, but he is."

It seemed a shocking thing to say – Connie had expected it to shock Frank. But he just shrugged and shook his head and said: "Maybe so, Mouse. But what can *I* do about it?"

She had no answer to that. It was just a matter of personality, she'd come to think. Frank and Johnny were different, that was all. She had to hope it wouldn't always be that way.

Annie, she felt, was more resilient. A tomboy. Good at sports, like Frank. More like him than Johnny was, to tell the truth.

And a girl, besides. Exempt from the demands fathers made on sons.

Meanwhile, Connie tried to help. If Frank was stretched under the truck on a piece of cardboard, bolting in some heavy, greasy part, she sent Johnny out to hand him tools. If Frank was sawing boards on the back porch, she sent Johnny out to learn how you measured first with a steel tape, then drew a pencil line to saw by. All the things George had done with *her* father. Didn't boys like that? Of course they did. And she was sure Johnny would have liked it too, if only Frank hadn't been so ... *angry*. The boy had inherited some of her clumsiness. His gaze would wander; his hand would slip. Frank would yell at him, and Johnny would steal away as soon as he could.

Before long, he didn't want to go out there at all. But she made him.

"Of *course* he wants you," she would say as brightly as she could. "And he needs your help. He really does."

Because Johnny was a boy. He couldn't be a baby forever.

That's how Connie usually thought, and how she would think again. It wasn't the fault of the spanking – what little there was of *that*. It was Johnny himself. He had to get tougher.

But not now. Now she lay in a misery of sweat and shame; her head throbbed. She remembered how Johnny had sneaked up after lunch and hugged her. Poor kid. And she remembered what Frank had said in front of Annie. It seemed to her that nothing had changed since four years ago when Nellie Ames Weldon came and the rain fell endlessly outside and the walls smelled of mildew and she cowered in this same bed, certain of her worthlessness as a mother. As a wife. As a human being.

When Tommy woke up, she was crying.

She carried him into the bathroom and wiped her eyes with a towel and found the bottle of aspirin. Then she carried him into the hallway and phoned the crew dispatcher again.

No, they hadn't seen Frank. But his crew was third out now.

23.

Almost everybody was at Hughie's clubhouse: John and Annie, Gary and Jimmy, Hughie and his brother Walt, even Jackpot Sykes. The others were climbing onto the roof, screaming and swinging from the branches of the willow trees like monkeys. (What would Pastor Johnson say about that?) At first John was nervous around Gary, whose face with those pale, squinty eyes didn't show whether he was mad or not. *And maybe he* should *be mad*, John thought. *I invited him in, after all.* Now and then he glanced across the street to see if his father's truck had returned.

He took off his shirt again.

He knew he wasn't supposed to. His mother had said so; Gary had heard her. But if he disobeyed, maybe Gary would think that he was brave – that they were both on the same side, even. Maybe Gary wouldn't feel so bad about what she'd said to *him*.

Whose side *was* John on?

He didn't know. All he knew was, it excited him to take his shirt off, with everybody watching ... just because he *wasn't* supposed to.

Then he was swinging in the willows too. And screaming like Gary.

Ten feet above ground, John jumped for a branch and slipped. He barely caught it with one hand, then with both. Kicking wildly. An explosion of fear. The branch cracked but held. The shock of relief came just as a cloud drifted over Mt. Bradley from the west. A thunderhead. It only half blocked the sun; just formed a bruise-dark background for the green-and-gold light shining through the willow leaves. At that moment, as if through a magnifying glass, he saw how every scratch in the smooth gray trunk revealed the moist green inner bark, the white wood; he saw cedar branches nearby -- not leaves, not needles, but a network of scaly fingers – glowing like velvet. In the sudden coolness he heard bird calls that must have been going on all the time. John shivered. There were goose pimples all over his skin. And then, unexpectedly, the joy came back. He was an Indian again. He felt the strain of hanging from the branch run like fire down from his arms into his body. He remembered the fort and his thoughts of torture, but that wasn't all of it; there was something else his body longed for, something he couldn't even name....

He wished Julie Land still lived there.

# # # #

Then they went down past the blackberry bushes, picking a few berries that were ripe, and wound up at Hughie's sandbox, pouring in water and floating chips of wood. Hughie looked worried, the way Jimmy had looked when Gary climbed the steps to the Hillers' house. "We'd better turn it off," he kept saying. But nobody listened to him. Gary just grabbed the hose and turned up the water higher and sprayed it until the sandbox became a lake, with big waves running.

"Stop that," Hughie said.

"It's a hurricane!" Gary yelled. "Hurricane!"

"My mom says – "

But nobody listened. Hughie just wasn't the kind of guy anybody listened to. He was as tall as Gary, but skinnier – his ribs showed, and his chest was as pale as John's. His eyes and hair were dark. Over his right eye, running into his hair, was a splotch of reddish purple – a birthmark. Maybe that was it. Because there wasn't anything else wrong with Hughie that John could see, yet everybody seemed to know. Just like they knew about Gary, the opposite way. Even when Hughie got mad, like now, he didn't scare anybody.

Then Gary turned the hose straight up, so that it seemed to be raining. "Hurricane, hurricane!" he chanted. Annie squealed. Sand was stuck in a circle to the seat of her jeans. Hughie grabbed for the hose and water flew everywhere, rattling against windowpanes and the faded peach-colored siding of the house. Gary sprayed him in the face. Walt ducked. Jackpot Sykes hooted, his limp arm flapping.

"I'm gonna tell my mom!" Hughie yelled. John couldn't tell if he was crying or not, with all the water dripping from his hair.

"She's not your mom," John said scornfully – still riding the good feeling he'd had in the willows, still on Gary's side, joining the laughter. "Your mom's gone."

Then Hughie's grandmother was right behind him. She had burst out the back door. Her face was white with powder, her mouth thin and red; her upper lip (he thought at that instant) was wrinkled like the cowcatcher on an old locomotive. She threw up her hands as if shooing away a flock of birds. Then she rushed to the spigot – knocking off the lid of the garbage can so that it rang, spinning, on the walk – and turned off the water. She looked up. Her red lips opened; her eyes, outraged, were focused on him, John. She was saying:

"You shut up. Get out of here!"

John's throat clenched.

"Filthy kids. All of you. I *told* you not to play with water."

"We didn't do nothin', " Gary said.

"*You,*" she said to John. "Don't you *ever* talk like that. I don't want to see you around here anymore."

She reached for Hughie, who was as slippery as a fish.

# # # #

Then they were running, east of Jackpot's house and north of Dr. Malevich's, to where the bulldozers had been working on the freeway.

Dirt was piled up in long ridges. The prints of huge treads – like tanks'? – seemed to be hammered into the ground, deeply shadowed. The men had stopped working for the day. It was quiet. Little red flags hung from lines of wooden stakes.

"They'd make good spears," Gary said.

He didn't seem to be bothered at all. But then, it wasn't really because of Gary that Hughie's grandmother had gotten so mad. It was mostly John's fault.

"What happened?" Annie kept asking. "What did you do?"

"I didn't do anything," John said. "She's crazy. Old witch."

But he knew what he'd done. What he'd said.... He just didn't know why.

Children can be very cruel, his mother had said.

But he hadn't meant to be cruel. It was just.... He'd felt good for a moment.

Every time I feel good, he thought, *something happens.*

We've sinned, Gary had said.

But now Gary was yelling "Ungawa! Ungawa!" and jumping up and down. Jimmy had found some half-gallon milk cartons in Dr. Malevich's garbage. He lined them up on one of the ridges of dirt. They were supposed to be African natives now, spearing their enemies. Or lions.

"Ungawa!" they all yelled.

The cartons were hard to hit, though. The stakes weren't balanced right to throw. Dully, John remembered that he'd used the same kind of stake to make his sword. *Death is better than dishonor*. It seemed so stupid. He glanced down at his chest – it was sunburned now, but still sickly-looking – and wished he could put his shirt back on. But then he wouldn't look like a native.

"Where's your bow and arrows?" he asked Jackpot.

"Broke 'em." Jackpot said, showing his rotten teeth. He didn't seem to care. "All three of 'em."

"The arrows? Jeez, already?"

Jackpot shrugged.

I thought so, John thought. The dirt didn't look much like Africa, either. More like a reddish-yellow desert, striped by shadows and glare. His stomach felt queasy again. He saw how the bulldozers had scraped an angle from Rodley's Ford dealership north to the bridge over the river, bypassing the S turn on Highway 99. He remembered the big truck that had flipped over on that turn in the spring. That's where they all flipped over, after they lost their brakes on the long grade down from Mount Shasta City. This one had slid all the way off the road into somebody's front yard. It rested on its side in a haze of dust, some of its double wheels turning slowly, the surprisingly thin metal skin of the trailer torn open. John saw the driver climb out of the cab, a little blood on his forehead, and argue with a policeman who had just driven up. John was too far away to hear them, but he saw the driver step forward suddenly and throw his arms out. Then the policeman punched him in the jaw – *bang!*

Knocked him down.

Now John thought about how hard it must be to punch somebody in the jaw. In real life, not the movies. With his sweaty face moving and his jaw just a slippery point your fist had to hit if you didn't want him to hit back.

John wondered if *he* could do it. What he would need. Practice? *Clean living?*

But his mother had been angry at the policeman, Mr. Brettschneider. "He had no right," she said. "The man was probably in shock. He might have been injured. Who knows? And Pete Brettschneider had his gun and his nightstick – it's not as if he was in any danger."

It was only when she spoke that John had remembered how much the driver's face, thin and yellow, had looked like Ronnie Knudson's.

His father had just said: "They ought to straighten out that damn turn. Brian down at the Texaco was telling me, one of those truck drivers told *him*, 'Mister, we hate to drive through your town.' At the bottom of the hill like that, no runaway lane, no place to bail out."

But how could anybody hate Dunsmuir?

Then he saw Freddie Ordoñez coming from the direction of Hughie's house. Freddie hesitated at the edge of the dirt, as if afraid to join them. His shadow stretched out. He had something in his right hand, the bright pink of mercurochrome. A squirt gun? John turned to wave him over before he disappeared again. He wanted to tell Freddie he was sorry ... for leaving him back in the woods, for going along with the Jap business. He remembered how Hughie's face had looked when Gary squirted him with the hose. Had John made Freddie's face look like that? The same way Gary's face had looked for a minute or two in the Hillers' kitchen? The way Cleo's face had looked when John stuck her with the dart? Or Annie's face when he claimed she hadn't caught the fish? Or Hughie's grandmother's face....

It all whirled together in that sick place in John's stomach. It was all his fault.

He remembered the truck driver's face at the moment the fist hit it.

"Hey!" he shouted.

John took two steps, and the next thing he knew he was running between the trees in Hughie's back yard, the low sun flashing through them like spokes. Later he would wonder if he'd set a world record for the 100-yard dash, with nobody there to click the stopwatch. What had happened to him seemed to unreel backward. He thought he saw, for the first time, Curly McPherson walking slowly up through the poison oak to his house, a gray-headed man in overalls, carrying a black lunch box. But he would never be sure he hadn't imagined it.... Then he saw little Walt trotting after him for a while, looking gravely interested. Then Annie's shocked mouth, like an O. And finally the spear clattering away after it had stuck him in the leg.

Had it?

Then the street. He was flying up the front steps to his house – as smoothly as on those escalators in Sacramento; his feet never seemed to touch.

24.

"It was Jimmy," Annie said, still breathless. "Jimmy Grissom did it."

"I don't know," John said. "I can't remember."

He knew he was in big trouble. He'd gotten hurt, and that meant a trip to the doctor, and that meant a doctor bill to pay. He was even dirtier now – his mother grimaced as she tried to pull off his jeans. And if Hughie's grandmother ever told her about what John had said, it would be twice as bad. His father might use the hairbrush then. A good thing Frank Hiller wasn't home yet. No truck.

"It's your fault as much as Jimmy's," his mother said. "Playing with such dangerous things.... Johnny, sit still. At least take that darn gun belt off."

She unbuckled it and slid the jeans down to his knees. The hole was in the middle of his right thigh. There wasn't much blood – just what looked like yellowish lumps of fat inside. Around it, the skin was paler than usual, and faintly mottled.

"Would you look at this?" she said. "The point didn't even go through the cloth. Just sort of stuffed it down in there."

He was in trouble – but, he realized, he was safe, too. He'd gotten hurt; his mother wouldn't punish him on top of that. Not now, anyway.

And she was still waiting for his father to return. Or call. *Something.* John sensed that her mind was mostly on that – not on his spear wound. Any other time, that would have bothered him – he was just a kid! He'd been stabbed! – but now it helped.

"Does it hurt?" his mother asked.

"It stings a little."

"I'll call Dr. Reed. I'm sure it's going to need stitches. And maybe a tetanus shot, too."

"Does *she* have to watch?" John said, meaning Annie. It embarrassed him, sitting in the living room in just his shorts.

"Oh, for Pete's sake," his mother said. But she told Annie, who pouted: "Go see what Tommy's up to." And then to John: "I'd better take you down there. Let me get some gauze."

"I can't go swimming again?" he asked.

"Probably."

He remembered when he was seven years old – they'd just moved from Sacramento Avenue – and he and his mother were walking downtown to buy the family's season ticket for the community pool next to the ballpark. It cost five dollars. She had stayed on the sidewalk while he cut across a vacant lot. He tripped over a root and fell on some trash and broken whiskey bottles. The hard clay scraped his right hand. It seemed on fire, unbearable. Crying, flapping it in the air to cool it, he ran to his mother, who looked at him with sudden intensity and grabbed the *other* hand, which hadn't hurt at all. Then he saw. His wrist gaped open; inside were red and bluish cords. His mother fumbled a handkerchief out of her purse – in seconds soaked with blood. He heard her breathing. "Hold it up," she said harshly. As in a dream, they were right across the street from Dr. Reed's office. She held his left hand up as they jaywalked; he was still flapping the right hand. In Dr. Reed's waiting room he felt dizzy, and wondered if they'd have to wait a long time on his maplewood chairs by the magazine rack, but the nurse knew right away they were in a hurry....

Now his mother taped the gauze to his leg and dialed Dr. Reed. When she was done, she said, "Put your shirt on," but she didn't ask why he'd had it off again.

# # # #

Dr. Reed was ready for them. He used the same oddly curved needle and the same blue-black thread: three stitches in John's leg, the same as in the wrist. He said the same thing about swimming: "Not until we get those stitches out, at least. There's too much risk of infection. You've got the whole town swimming in there -- no telling what kind of crud." Dr. Reed had a forehead as high as Dr. Chenoweth's, but instead of being smooth and impassive it wrinkled up like a sheet of corrugated roofing tin as his eyebrows lifted. He had a dry way of talking that made John's mother laugh. She liked Dr. Reed; he'd gone to Cal too. "That man has no bedside manner at *all,*" she would say, "unless you're *really* sick." John liked him OK, except during physicals when Dr. Reed checked him with his shorts off. "Bag of worms," he'd always say, fingering John's left testicle. It hung lower than the right one, and seemed shriveled, and inside were the outlines of bluish things like those John had glimpsed inside his wrist. Dr. Reed never said what it meant. Just "bag of worms."

But this time, though John had to take his pants down, Dr. Reed didn't say it. He just leaned back, crossing his knees and lacing his hands over the top one, amid the sharp smell of antiseptic and the gleam of his chrome-plated instruments, and asked, "How did this ... ah, puncture happen?"

When John didn't answer, his mother said: "Playing African natives. I think."

"African natives." Dr. Reed nodded. "That'll do it every time."

# # # #

Years later, his mother would tell John something else about Dr. Reed: how when Tommy had gotten so sick just after he was born – so sick he might die – Dr. Reed had broken down and wept in front of her. Still a youngish man, not so many years out of medical school, a Dunsmuir boy who had come back to practice in his home town. Connie Hiller had never seen a doctor cry before or since. She didn't blame him, as far as John could tell. She believed he'd done everything a doctor in Oakland could have done. And it wasn't exactly that he seemed to feel guilty about it, but from then on Dr. Reed took a special interest in how Tommy was getting along. He would often praise her: "You're doing a terrific job with him." She would protest that she wasn't doing anything any other mother wouldn't do. "Still," Dr. Reed would say.

Today all John noticed was how, before they left, Dr. Reed took his mother aside and spoke to her quietly, more like a friend than a doctor.

"How's Frank?" he asked.

She looked quickly at John to tell him: *Don't say anything.*

"Better, I think. It's an awful bruise. I – "

"I'd like him to come in and let me look at it again. At least before he goes back to work."

"That's the problem," Connie Hiller said. "They keep *calling* him. They won't let him alone to heal up. I wish – "

Dr. Reed frowned. "That's not good," he said. And it seemed to John that he was about to say something more – something bad about the Southern Pacific? – and changed his mind.

"Frank gets so *angry* about it," she said. "I can't help but worry."

"That's only natural," Dr. Reed said. But he spread his hands and shrugged as if to say nothing could be done. "Please. Have him get in touch."

John still held his breath, but that was all.

They drove home. His mother was silent; her hands gripped the wheel tightly. The sun had gone over the western mountains, but Girard Ridge still had a band of light on it. The air through the rolled-down windows was cooler. The hole in his leg didn't hurt much – it never would, even with the stitches in it. The sunburn on his chest was beginning to hurt more.

And there, in front of the house, as if it had never left, was his father's truck.

25.

Time sneaked up on Frank Hiller. It had seemed he had all day to stand and smoke and watch the switch engines in the yards put together a new train. Almost a hundred cars, with a second locomotive at the rear to help push them up the Cantara Loop grade. Tim Frulan's crew. Another of the old masters. After this freight headed north, Jamison would be second out ... and it *was* Jamison he'd seen by the crew dispatcher, he knew now. No matter how blurred his sight had been. He had a lot of explaining to do to a lot of people – he was beginning to realize just how much. He wouldn't live this day down anytime soon, not in Dunsmuir.

Then he noticed thunderclouds moving in. The sun was already going over the crags. At this time of year there were still hours of twilight left, but you never saw a real sunset here, or a dawn; the canyon was too steep and narrow. In winter the shadows fell at 3 p.m. It was good country, Frank had thought when he first came – good hunting and fishing country – but the lack of sky had bothered him. The mountains seemed to close over his head ... and never more than now, when his time had run out.

Trapped.

He had to call the Trainmaster. Right away, before Ross' office closed at five.

No way he could go back to the depot, looking like this. And there wasn't a pay phone he could use.

So he had to call from home, and that meant getting there the shortest and quickest way he knew how. Straight up the highway through the middle of town.

He was tired by now, and ashamed of himself, as he'd known he would be when he first drove away from the front of the house. *Falling.* If Connie were with him now, he'd tell her how sorry he was. He felt like a fool – going off half-cocked like that, without a plan. But when he climbed onto the truck's seat, he discovered that his back had stiffened up, and the pain made him angry all over again. How had he managed to drive so far? How the hell could anybody expect him to go to work? Once he'd started up and shifted into second gear, he left it there – no more need for the clutch. He half turned so that his weight rested on the side of his right leg, on the edge of the bruise. That way the pain was steady, almost bearable. Up Florence Avenue again, past the stores: he tried not to see any of it. Behnke was still at the Texaco pumps. Neither of them waved. Frank passed the point where he'd turned down to the tracks and the river – completing a circle. He ached in new places, twisted sideways like this. He stank of sweat. On the seat, on the dash, the mirror, were spots of dried blood. Still chipping away at the boulder in his gut, piece by piece, he wondered: *What do I tell Connie and the kids?*

But Connie's car was gone.

And as Frank stumbled up the front steps, he was certain she'd left *him*. Children were shouting somewhere across the street, but the house was silent.

He burst in, panting.

Where did she go? Back to Oakland? She took the kids with her?

For he deserved it, he knew. He deserved to be left alone.

It was a terrible moment, but then Cleo surged up around his legs, barking, and in the back bedroom he found Annie and Tommy with a Dr. Seuss book.

"Where's your mother?" Frank asked.

"She took Johnny to the doctor," Annie said. "She said she'd be right back."

"Johnny? What happened to *him*?"

"Jimmy Grissom speared him. In the leg."

"Speared?" None of this made any sense. "But she's coming home?"

"We were playing natives," Annie said. Then she noticed the blood on his shirt, his swollen nose. "Where'd *you* go, Daddy?"

"Oh, nowhere." He started to wave the question away, but this was his little girl, bound to him by an unbreakable thread of brightness, not Behnke. What *had* he said to her when he left? "I had to go down to the yards. Had to check on things."

Tommy, too, was staring at him.

"I just hit my head on something," Frank said. "Had to stop too fast. Nothing to worry about."

He left them, found a clean T-shirt and put the bloody shirt into the hamper. Then he picked it out and tossed it into the trash. He never wanted to see the thing again, even if it could be cleaned. Cleo stayed alongside, nosing at him until he stopped to pet her. "You missed me, girl? Huh? You missed me?" She licked his hand. For some reason, it mattered a lot that Cleo was glad to see him. How could he have gone off without the dog? It was hard to imagine now.

His back kept stiffening. Frank checked his watch and the angle of the light. He shook his head and sighed, leaned his elbow against the wall of the hallway and dialed Ross.

He knew what to expect. The Trainmaster would accept his apology. But there would be a price to pay. Oh, yes. This was just the beginning.

What Ross said to him, again, Frank never told anybody.

But when he hung up, it seemed much later, the evening air darker, though he couldn't have been on the phone more than five minutes. He was breathing hard. Those dogs had never quit whining next door.

Cleo was beside him – and, surprisingly, so was Annie. Her eyebrows under the cowboy hat were level. Had she overheard? Or was she still mad at him from this morning?

"Look, honey," he began.

"Did you see it?"

"What?"

"Did you see me catch my *fish*?"

Had she caught one? *Damn.* He couldn't remember. She'd been standing up on that rock across the river when he turned away. Had it happened right then?

"You were there!" she said. "I saw you!"

"Sure I saw you," Frank said, but he wasn't sure if she believed him. "Saw you reel it right in there. A heckuva job."

"It's in the fridge. You've gotta see it. Mom said she's gonna cook it for me."

So he followed her into the kitchen and looked at the trout.

'What'd you catch it with?" he asked.

"Huh?"

"What bait?"

"A salmon egg."

Frank nodded. "Well, that's great." His voice sounded strained. He was afraid she could tell he was lying. In the refrigerator was a fifth of Old Crow; he dragged it out by the neck and poured himself a shot. It tasted good – took the edge off all his aches. *Damn.* Maybe that's what he'd needed all along.

"How old were you when you caught *your* first fish?" Annie asked.

"Older than you," he told her. "Don't worry. You're the champ."

But he didn't want to talk anymore. Not to anybody. He wanted another drink, and he would have poured one, maybe, if Connie's car hadn't pulled up outside.

26.

"Well, I called him," Frank said. "I'm going out. Damned if I know how, but I'm going."

"You ... apologized to Mr. Ross?"

"I said so, didn't I? Isn't that what you wanted?"

"I wanted you *safe,*" Connie Hiller said.

She didn't know what to think. His nose was cut. How had that happened? He had whiskey on his breath. He was still angry ... but at least he was home.

Connie had been light-headed with relief ever since she saw the truck out front. Then Annie had run out and shouted, "Daddy's back!" It would have been enough to make her forget how Frank had been in the morning – except that he hadn't changed: He still seemed to be blaming her. *Isn't that what you wanted?* No, she thought. Not at all ... but what *did* she want?

Now Frank was lying on his stomach again, on the bed. He had taken off his shoes but not the rest of his clothes. "You might as well," she told him – if he was going to work, he would have to wear overalls anyway. How soon would the crew dispatcher call him? He was second out now, apparently. But Frank only grunted – out of spite, or was he hurting so much? "Do you want me to put something on that cut?" she asked. "You should see Johnny's leg. I had to bandage that up. What a day! I should get my nursing license." She waited for Frank to smile at that, to say *something* that would make things easier, but he didn't, so she went into the kitchen to start dinner. Fried chicken. That was simple enough; the chicken was thawed already, and the children loved it. Connie knew that Frank didn't like chicken much, but she was angry enough herself – how she'd *worried!* She hadn't heard anything from him all day – not to care. String beans and corn on the cob. Those were simple too. But first, before the dew got to them, she had to take down the clothes she'd hung out back. She wouldn't even bother to fold them, she decided – just pile them in the basket. That would get her out of the house for a few minutes. Clear her head.

She wished she'd had time to take a bath.

Horses sweat. Men perspire....

"Go show your dad what happened to *you*," she told Johnny.

He gave her a frightened look, and she remembered what she'd thought an hour or two ago – that she hadn't protected him enough. But that thought was already fading. What harm could *this* do?

"Go ahead," she said. "Show him. Chin up."

# # # #

John started changing the moment he saw the truck. All the strength went out of his arms and legs, as if the maroon paint and the dusty tires gave off a killer ray like kryptonite. His stomach lurched. It didn't matter how he'd felt lying in the fort, or swinging from that willow tree – how he'd dreamed about being brave. He couldn't help it now. He was in *big* trouble, with his safety gone – a coward and a sneak, tiptoeing up the steps, hoping his father was back in the bedroom, hoping he wouldn't ever come out.

Had Hughie's grandmother called?

Apparently not. Nobody said anything about that. And his father *was* in bed. Right away, John began planning: after dinner, how to slip past him to his own bedroom, shut the door, pull the covers over his head and pretend to be asleep.

But then his mother said, "Go show your dad what happened to *you.*"

He gave her a look – pleading with her – but it did no good.

His father lay on the bed in his brown slacks and a T-shirt. The Hawaiian shirt was gone. He was smoking a cigarette; as John peered in, he reached over the side of the bed and stubbed it into an ashtray on the floor. Cleo was there, curled up by his father's big shoes. *She loves him*, John thought. *Of course. She loves him the most.* It was dim in the room; his father's body threw a shadow on the wall, and seemed huge. John was still changing. For the first time since the spear had hit him, he felt dizzy. He might throw up.

Would that help, if he was *really* sick?

Frank Hiller raised his head. He said nothing at first – fishing another cigarette from a pack of Chesterfields beside the ashtray, tapping the end of it on the floor, striking flame from his silver Zippo, breathing in so that the end of the cigarette glowed orange. John had seen this so many times. Under the bitter smell of the smoke was a rank, heavy smell of grown man's sweat. John tried to look anywhere but into his father's eyes, but everything he did see – the muscles of his father's back, the creases of his neck, the dark-red scab on the side of his nose – only scared him more.

He wanted to run. But he was paralyzed.

"What's this about Jimmy spearing you?" his father said.

"It was an accident."

"But you were doing something dumb, right? What'd he spear you *with*?"

"A stake. A wood one. From the freeway." John began to pull down his pants. If he had any safety at all, it was in *proving* he was hurt. "It's got three stitches."

"Never mind. Don't mess with that bandage."

John stopped, bent over.

"It doesn't matter. The *point* is, it was dumb. Goddamn it..... *Look* at me. Whatever Jimmy did, it doesn't change the fact. Right? You weren't using your head."

John still couldn't look at him. The sickness rose from his stomach to his throat.

"Right?"

He pulled his pants up, but what good would that do? His father would grab him by the ear now, twist it so that it stung, and walk him into the bathroom where the hairbrush was....

But maybe this time, John realized, his father didn't want to get up. Maybe it would hurt *him* too much.

Lucky.

He let himself think, just for a moment, of what it would be like if his father were like Mr. Sykes. He could ask: *How'd you hurt your nose?* And they might even laugh together a little. At having both done dumb things on the same day.

But what if his father had been in a fight? Not with Mr. Grissom, but with somebody else.

Suppose he'd *lost?* John didn't dare ask.

Should he tell him about the arrowhead?

Instead, John heard himself say, "I saw Curly!", and saw by his father's face that he should have kept quiet.

"So?"

"He never ... comes out. I never saw him before."

"He comes out every day, for Chrissake." His father shook his head in disgust. "At least your brother's got an excuse. What's yours?"

# # # #

Was it possible to dislike your own kid? Frank Hiller wondered after John had ducked out of the room. He had never put the question to himself quite like that before, but once he did, he decided: *Yeah. Maybe.* It was a hell of a thing to say – he watched the cigarette smoke curl up in the air and form loops, as if it would spell out letters and words, tell him it wasn't so, of course it wasn't – but the boy was just too much like Ralph. For whatever reason. Frank couldn't help being bothered by it. The kid seemed to wear a "kick me" sign on his butt, and even when you didn't give in to the temptation, you were aware of having to resist it. And then when you *did* kick him, so to speak, you felt like shit. So wasn't that Johnny's own fault, in a way?

Frank didn't know.

Hell, getting speared ... not that he'd tell Johnny about it, but Frank had done dumb stuff like that when *he* was a kid, and survived. The problem was Johnny himself – how to go on raising him, a boy he didn't understand, probably never would. And Tommy. How to shoulder the burden of them all, his whole family, after he'd nearly put it down.

Like eating potatoes. Nothing but potatoes.

That's how life was going to be, now that he'd called the Trainmaster.

No way out.

Connie was cooking now. Frying some chicken, by God. Frank could hear the sizzle in the frying pan; then he could smell it. She knew he didn't like chicken. *She's still pissed at me*, he thought. This was just her way of rubbing it in.

# # # #

The fish on Annie's plate looked totally different now. Smaller. Her mother had rolled it in flour and fried it, so that its sides were crusty and brown. Its single eye was cooked white. She tried to remember how it had looked when it was alive and shiny, wiggling over the gravel. But she couldn't.

The fish was less than dead now. It was food.

"I almost fell off that rock," Annie said, and her mother, as always, took it wrong.

"You be *careful*. I don't know if I should let you ... you're so young."

"Mom."

Still, she was the only one at the table eating trout. Everybody else had chicken – and she could have chicken too, if she wanted. That made her special. They were watching her – jealous Johnny, and Tommy in his high chair. The vegetables steamed in their bowls. Her mother served them. Annie was just breaking the skin of the fish, trying to separate the tender white meat from the bones with her fork, when Cleo came out of her father's bedroom and barked. Then somebody knocked at the front door.

It was Jimmy Grissom.

# # # #

He wore a white shirt and black slacks with suspenders. Connie Hiller had never seen either of the Grissom boys dressed up before. Jimmy's face was white too, against the dusk outside, the skin stretched tight over his cheekbones. His hair was wet and slicked straight back, so that it seemed as if he'd run wide-eyed through a strong wind. And just as if he'd run, he had no voice left. "My pa says ... he already whupped me," Jimmy whispered. "He says ... he says you can do what you want."

"Come in, Jimmy," Connie said.

"I'm sorry, ma'am." He didn't look at Johnny, who came up beside her with Cleo. "It was an accident."

"So we heard."

Jimmy shuffled his feet. "I gotta go to church soon."

"You don't want a bite? We've got plenty."

"No, ma'am. We already et. My pa says...."

"Oh, come on in, Jimmy. Sounds as if you've already been punished enough." She called in to the bedroom: "Frank! Jimmy Grissom's here. He came to apologize."

Frank grunted.

"I know you're tired and sore, but he's come all the way up here just to say he's sorry." The sympathy Connie had felt for Johnny was transferred now to this other little boy, who looked so guilty and woebegone, not like his brother at all.

Frank signed and grumbled, but he finally came out.

"I guess he'll live," Frank said, meaning Johnny. "You play with sharp sticks, that's what happens. I told *him* it was dumb, and I guess Charley told you too, right?"

"Yessir."

"Well, what's more to say? You want something to eat?"

# # # #

John was happy to see Jimmy – didn't blame him at all for being speared. All he could remember, still, was the stake falling away and Annie's startled face. Jimmy had made him safe, he thought – had taken the whipping for him. John remembered how Annie had walked bowlegged over to Dr. Malevich's, holding that five-dollar bill; then how Mr. Grissom had tossed the toolbox into the trunk of his car this morning, the muscles like rawhide under his shirt. He must have used a belt, John thought. A leather belt. *Poor Jimmy. He's sorer than I am, probably....*

And now Jimmy was safe too, though he didn't seem to realize it yet, edging over the worn linoleum into the Hillers' kitchen. A bubble of safety surrounded him wherever he went. "See the fish I caught?" Annie said. Tommy was talking to himself, as usual. John's mother was smiling. Cleo wagged her tail. And his father, even, was trying to be nice, standing in the doorway to the hall with his head tilted, giving off that smell of whiskey and sweat. John had the sudden, strange feeling that he was spying on his parents – as if Jimmy had taken his place just when they decided to show how good and kind they could be. He was proud of them at that moment – proud of his whole family – and jealous, too. Jimmy was somebody else's kid. That's what made him safe.

"Where'd you catch it?" Jimmy asked.

"Down under the bridge," Annie said.

"I wish *I* could go fishing," Jimmy said, and John wondered: *Hasn't he gone before? Don't Okies know how?*

"Clyde took me," Annie said. "Maybe – " She had eaten most of the fish already, except for the head and tail.

John said: "You want a drumstick?"

"Jimmy said he already had dinner," his mother said. "But how about a little ice cream? We've got Neapolitan."

# # # #

Connie Hiller was glad, too, that Jimmy had come. It was a chance for her to make up for getting upset at Gary at lunch. And it surprised her that Frank actually had come out, despite his pain, and talked to the boy. Been civil to him. It was what she'd been waiting for, she realized. The first sign of his old self. Connie warmed to him – now that he'd done what she wanted, called the Trainmaster, she could let herself feel all over again that what the railroad was doing to Frank was worse than wrong. It was criminal. *No wonder he was angry. Who could blame him?* She could forget, at the moment, that he still hadn't told her where he'd been most of the day, or how he'd gotten that cut on the side of his nose. *It's too much. What can they expect a flesh-and-blood person to stand?* A little of her headache had lingered all this time; now it faded at last. She moved toward him, bringing him a plate and a fork so he could eat standing up.

# # # #

Annie had no doubt her father had seen her catch the fish. He'd said so, hadn't he? *You're the champ.* And it had tasted so good – especially the skin, with butter and salt on it. She only wished it had been bigger, and that Jimmy could have seen it fresh-caught. Then he would have been jealous too.

Jimmy looked so funny in his starched white shirt; with his hair combed back, the top inch of his forehead was a pale stripe above the tan. Annie was a little in awe of him. What was it like to spear a person, not just a milk carton? Only Jimmy knew. Annie was glad the spear hadn't hurt Johnny much. But why hadn't it stuck? That's what she wanted to know. If it made a hole like that, it should have gone right through his jeans and stuck in his leg, like the hook in the fish's jaw. Shouldn't it?

# # # #

Frank Hiller had to respect Charley Grissom. He'd done the right thing, even if it was hard on the kid. That made it easy for him, Frank – he could let Jimmy off with just a word to the wise, and even grin, saying, "He should've kept out of the line of fire." Meaning Johnny. Going to church on Wednesday nights as well as Sundays – that was taking things to an extreme, as far as Frank was concerned. But maybe there was something to it. Those Grissom boys had been taught their manners; you had to admit that.

Connie had given Jimmy a dish of ice cream and tucked a towel in the neck of his shirt for a bib. Now she took the end of the towel and wiped the corners of his mouth. "There," she said. "Was that good?"

"Yes, ma'am." Jimmy shuffled again. "Thank you, ma'am ... for everything. But I gotta go now."

"Well, don't let us keep you, Jimmy," Connie said. "Have a good time."

"Yes, ma'am.... Sir."

Then Jimmy was gone, and the whole feeling in the house changed back to what it had been before. Frank stood holding the plate of chicken, corn and beans. He looked at the too-big living room with not enough furniture in it, a second-hand couch and a carpet with a worn spot in the middle; then he glanced back in to the bedrooms with their unfinished walls. It made no sense to keep working on the house, but he knew he would anyway. They might not have to move for a year or two; the freeway project was so slow. And even though the house would have to be demolished – it was too high above the street to be jacked onto a mover's truck, even if he'd *want* to move the damn thing -- he would keep hammering and painting on it. Like the sucker he was.

Twice today he had driven through downtown Dunsmuir and hardly recognized it. Now his own home seemed equally strange. He'd left it – in his mind, anyway. Left it for good. Now he didn't belong in it. But here he was.

Trapped.

Frank limped into the kitchen, where the kids froze with their spoons over *their* ice cream. Only Tommy was still happy, rocking in his high chair – and what a hell of a life *he* had waiting for him, Frank thought. A blessing Tommy had no way of knowing it. And Johnny. Frank fought against the idea that he didn't like the boy. A good student at least. Johnny got the grades ... but then, so had Ralph, and what good had it done *him*, all those straight As? Just a minute ago, joking with Jimmy, Frank had seen Johnny grin along with them. Brown-nosing. Frank hadn't been able to resist shooting him a look and seeing the grin die. Johnny *asked* for it. That was the truth. And you couldn't do that and survive in this life – not when somebody like Ross would be waiting for you. And there always *would* be a Ross, by God. That was the only exam that counted.

Frank ate his vegetables; he hardly touched the chicken. The greasy smell of it sickened him. He thought of an old family story: about Great-uncle Howard, who had joined the Klondike gold rush in 1898 and been stranded for the winter in a cabin on the Yukon, with snow up to the eaves and nothing but dried fish to eat. Howard Mullahy had eaten dried fish for six months straight; then he'd come home to Yuba City and never touched a fish again in his life. Frank could understand that. He'd *told* Connie about having to clean those coops ... just as he'd told her the other stories, about the SP and the land they'd lost. All for nothing.

He left the plate on the drainboard. He opened the refrigerator and took out the bottle of Old Crow and poured himself another shot. *Damn.* Then he took the bottle and the glass with him, heading back to bed.

# # # #

Frank didn't get drunk that night. Nor would he get drunk for more than twenty years to come. He would just drink a little more steadily than before. Connie would notice that the bottle in the refrigerator wouldn't last quite as long before another replaced it, but she wouldn't say anything; it wouldn't seem to matter. But in his fifties, his health would deteriorate. He would have his gall bladder removed at the SP Hospital in San Francisco; later he would lose part of his large intestine. Then he would drink more. By then he would be a conductor – as respected by the younger generation of brakemen as Jamison and Frulan had been by Frank's – though a conductor's job wouldn't be what it was: Computers would do more and more of the thinking and train crews would be controlled by radio from headquarters. Nor would Dunsmuir be the same. Interstate 5 would largely bypass the town. Stores on Florence Avenue would close, then stand vacant. (Time was, he would think, when you could stroll down that street and buy a Ford, a Dodge, a washing machine or a good suit of clothes; now you had to go to Redding or Yreka, fifty miles either way, to get such things.) The Commercial Garage, where Charley Grissom once worked, would collapse under snow and never be rebuilt. The population would dwindle. No longer needing a division point north of Roseville, the SP would pull out many of its facilities – the engine shops, the roundhouse. Frank, bored and restless, would do auditing work for his union – the old Brotherhood having merged into the United Transportation Union, just as the SP would soon be swallowed by the Union Pacific. Maybe management would hold that against him. Frank would think so. At any rate, his drinking would be noticed.

After his death, Connie would find a note, penned in his neat, firm handwriting on lined yellow paper. The end of it said: *I had to be Superman. That's what you all expected of me. I had to carry the full load, all the time. I just got worn out.*

# # # #

Now she said, "Frank, are you sure...."

"What?"

"Are you sure this is a good idea?"

He was lying on the bed – where she had lain this afternoon and felt so miserable. A dim, sprawled shape, with a red dot from his cigarette. His glass clinked.

"You think it matters now?"

"If you have to go to work – "

"Oh, I *have* to. You made damn sure of that."

It was as if being nice to Jimmy Grissom had taken the last bit of goodwill Frank had in him. Now he was shutting Connie out again. *Your language*, she wanted to say but caught herself. *The children*.

"*I* made you...?"

"Isn't it enough I'm down on my knees? Those sonsabitches are getting away with it? Huh? Now I can't even take a drink – in my own goddamn house."

In the morning, when they'd argued, they'd done it alone, or tried to. Not anymore.

"Frank, please."

"What?"

"Will you *stop* it?"

"Down on my goddamn knees. And you don't even know what that means."

"Frank – "

"Just leave me *alone*, will you?"

So Connie Hiller did – again with that numb feeling as if Frank had slapped her full in the face. She returned to the kitchen: to the crusted dishes, the chicken bones, the basket of unfolded laundry. *Tobacco Road*. Tommy had wet himself; she lifted him out of the high chair and took him to the bathroom and peeled off his pants and washed him and pulled on his pajamas while Cleo sniffed under the table for fallen scraps of food. "Shoo!" she told the dog, coming back with Tommy on her hip. He was falling asleep again. Boneless, his head on her shoulder. Johnny was in the living room, listening to the Lone Ranger. Annie helped her listlessly, passing plates.

Her despair came back.

The family's broken, Connie thought, even as she clutched Tommy to her.

27.

Earlier that day, John had been hypnotized by the pebbles and dirt in the back yard. Now it was the beige threads of the upholstery of one arm of the couch as he huddled next to the radio. And his skin. He looked at the pores on the backs of his hands, the pattern of the veins; it seemed strange, his skin, as if he'd never really seen it before. As if it belonged to somebody else. Or some other kind of animal. He looked at the scar on his wrist; then he glanced down the neck of his T-shirt at his sunburned chest, by now almost as bright a pink as Freddie Ordoñez's squirt gun. The hole in his leg hardly hurt. It just ached a little, below the surface. But his chest stung. It felt hot. That was where the dizzy feeling seemed to come from – the fever – as he overheard his parents' voices.

John tried to listen to the radio, with the volume turned down: *From out of the pages of yesteryear*, and then, as the William Tell Overture faded, the pounding of horses' hooves, the roar of six-guns and the Lone Ranger's voice, as deep as a roll of thunder. It was the same as ever, and yet somehow different. For the first time in his life he was bored with the Lone Ranger; for the first time (with that part of his mind that stood off to the side and watched) he could tell halfway through how the story would end. With a kind of shock, he began to suspect that nothing bad could happen to the Lone Ranger because the story had been written that way, and he wanted to change the story. Give the outlaws a chance. Even the preview of next week's episode, which left the Lone Ranger in a terrible fix – *We got 'im covered, boys! Now, let's just see who's behind that mask* – even that was a trick. For every week the Lone Ranger escaped.

Then, as the program ended, he heard real thunder. Just a grumble of it, off to the northwest. It wasn't close enough to make Cleo howl, but it bothered her, John could tell; he heard her feet clicking restlessly in the hall. "Here, girl," he called, and she came into the living room. "Good dog," he said and scrooched off the couch and sat on the floor beside her; he put his arms around her neck. "Good doggy," he chanted, the fever rising. Cleo trembled and whined. John told her he loved her – told her it was just noise; it couldn't hurt her – but she was deaf to him now, lost to her fear, jerking each time the thunder came.

28.

"Frank?"

He had been lying on his stomach again for a while, and he felt better. The whiskey helped. He had heard another northbound freight moan up the canyon – that meant he was first out. When would the call come? He should sleep all he could. But as it turned out, he wouldn't sleep; the call wouldn't come until midnight, and by then the bruise would be rigid again; he would begin to suspect that his nose was broken. It would be a real chore to drag himself to work – Connie would have to drive him to the depot, as she'd done in those old days, the honeymoon. It would be as hard to climb the steel steps of the caboose as he could imagine, and nothing after that would be any easier.

But now Frank felt better, listening to the thunder and a few big drops of rain. The air was cool, comfortable. Connie came in.

"Frank, those dogs next door ... Thelma's dogs. They're still barking. I've heard them all day, but we've just been so ... distracted. It's like she hasn't *fed* them or something. Could there be something wrong?"

And when Frank spoke, it was in his normal voice. "Yeah, I heard 'em too, this morning. I wondered what was eating 'em. Maybe you ought to go check."

"I wish *you* would. It's dark.... It's creepy over there."

"In the shape I'm in?"

He laughed – the same bitter sound he'd made that morning.

But the whiskey had soothed him just enough. He noticed the desperation in Connie's face, and it wasn't because she was afraid of the dark. No. She was offering this to him – the man's job. It wasn't that she couldn't do it herself.

"You were gone for *hours*," she said. "This is just next door."

Leaving home had given him power over her – over all of them. He saw that. It was why he had felt so good driving off in the truck, despite the shame of it. *Now, damn it, maybe you'll listen. Just once.* If he'd gone clear to Mexico, disappeared, they'd be paying attention forever. Even Ross might have felt bad about it, a little.

Sonsabitches.

Now the only power he had was to stay here, sulking, like a kid who didn't want to get out of bed on a cold morning and go to school.

And that was stupid, Frank felt now. That was childish. Even though he would never get justice from the Southern Pacific, and Connie would never come to him the way he wanted, with her hair unpinned and tears flowing – climbing into bed with him, murmuring, touching him softly and taking the pain away. Those days were over. Yet it had taken guts for Connie to come to him at all, he saw, after the way he'd snarled at her. To ask him – to offer him his place in the family back.

Togetherness.

Because that's what she was doing. Wasn't she?

It was time to knock the next chip off the boulder inside him.

"Well, OK, Mouse," he said. "Just hold on a minute. Let me put on my shoes."

He heard her sigh in relief.

Frank groaned as he swung his feet to the floor. Between thunderclaps he could hear Thelma Hoffman's dogs. Connie was right. They were going crazy over there.

"You ought to take a flashlight," Connie said.

He ignored her – the last of his defiance – even though he knew it was a good idea. He couldn't see well where he was limping in the back yard, through all that dogshit. The air smelled of ozone, though the thunder was fading now and the raindrops were widely spaced. The edge of the storm, nothing more. He turned between the houses and felt something squish under his left shoe. *Damn.* He climbed the creaky side steps to Thelma Hoffman's porch and paused. No light. He knocked on her door. There was no answering voice, but a flurry of animal sounds: yips, whines, the scrape of claws, the thud of little bodies trying to break through the wood and reach him.

"Thelma?" he called.

Nothing. Nothing human, anyway.

The door was unlocked. Frank turned the knob and pushed. It gave way; the dogs scrabbled in a frenzy, and a cat flashed out at his feet.

"Thelma? You there?"

Still no answer. Frank went in, and most of what happened next John would have to imagine, just as he would imagine so much of this day – what went on in his mother's mind, his sister's. All John would know for sure was that his parents argued twice; in between, his father drove off for hours; he came home with a cut and swollen nose. Then he went back to work, though the terrible bruise from the derailment hadn't healed yet. John would remember certain events: He got speared. Annie caught a fish. He would remember *fear*, if not the reasons for it. For what did his father do to him, after all? Nothing, or almost nothing.

We never asked you to be Superman.

When his mother discovered that note among his father's papers, John would still be "finding himself" after Vietnam, just as Ronnie Knudson had done after Korea.

Did we?

# # # #

What John would imagine is this: His father went into Thelma Hoffman's living room. It was dark, with the shades and curtains drawn. He couldn't find a light switch. The dogs swirled around him; the cats whipped in and out of his vision. He could feel something crunch on the hardwood floor underfoot. More turds? Dried dog food? Corners of furniture bumped him, and there was a powerful smell – the day's closed-in heat and spoiled canned cat food and unwashed clothes and rotten wood and stove grease and old-lady mustiness, all at once. A faucet dripped. Frank followed that sound. His eyes were still adjusting to the dark; the air seemed to swarm, as if bugs or even bats were circling his head. *I needed that flashlight after all, by God.* In what had to be Thelma's dining room, there was a table with her typewriter and stacks of papers on it, and a windowshade raised enough to show an inch of outdoor light. He used that light to lift the shade, and then he saw the switch at the entrance to the kitchen. That was where the faucet was. Still dripping. Plink, plop, plink. Frank turned on the light. The dogs barked louder – he could see them now: a dachshund, a Yorkie mix and a couple of Scotch terriers – and then he saw Thelma. She was lying on the kitchen floor, squares of gray linoleum, on her back with one knee raised, so he could see her fat leg with its purple varicose veins. She was wearing an old blue bathrobe, as if she'd just gotten up in the morning; she must have been trying to make a phone call when the stroke or whatever it was had hit.

Thelma had dragged the phone down with her as she fell. The receiver was on the floor, beeping along with the faint sounds she must have been making all day.

29.

"Creepy, all right," Frank said.

He was breathing hard again, John saw. He had called Frenchy Rubidoux's ambulance service from Thelma Hoffman's phone, and in ten minutes Frenchy had driven up from the south end of town. Frank had tried to help lift Thelma onto a stretcher and carry her down to the street, but his back hurt too much; Frenchy and his partner had had to do it all. Now Frank stood beside Connie and the kids in the flashing red light. She was talking to nobody in particular:

"She had such a hard time. I could cry. Remember when Thelma's mother was still alive? She was out of her head – she must have been eighty-five – and she'd just *curse* Thelma, like a sailor, and Thelma never complained, just took care of her all those years until she died. Do you remember?"

John didn't.

"We'd just moved in.... Just *cursed* her. I'll never forget it. Of course, the old lady didn't know what she was saying. But for Thelma.... She was really fond of you kids. I hope you knew that."

John hadn't known. All he knew about Thelma Hoffman was the fuzzy slippers, the tall glasses of iced tea (or whatever it was) and the smell of dog poop. This new fact about her didn't fit. Now she was dying

– everybody felt that, though she was still alive when they slid her into the ambulance. John couldn't see much – just her mottled bare feet and the curve of a cheek. She had a blanket over her.

Quite a crowd had gathered by then. None of the Grissoms – they were at church. And no Curly McPherson. But all three of the Sykes kids were there, with Mrs. Sykes, looking shy or dazed as usual, hanging back. Clyde came with Mrs. Knudson, a bony woman holding an unbuttoned red cardigan over her shoulders. Mrs. Ordoñez came with Freddie and his sisters, Nicole and Juana. The two Lorenzo kids, Paul and Vickie, came, with their perfect skin and long-lashed eyes. Paul couldn't have seen any more of Thelma Hoffman than John had, but he was already concocting the story that would make the rounds of the neighborhood in the next few days:

When they found her, she was all swoled up, and she was purple. She'd already started to rot. Those dogs, they got so hungry, they'd started to eat on her. Swear to God! They chewed off part of one of her arms. She couldn't move. She just had to lie there and watch 'em eat her....

None of this was true, John knew. But in time he would half believe it anyway. It was a better story.

Now some of those dogs were out on the street. Cleo had joined them. They sniffed one another's noses and hind ends; they ran in circles. They acted glad to be outside – just as the people watching the doors of the ambulance slam shut were glad to be alive and well, not like Thelma. The Hillers, especially, were horrified that Thelma had lain so long only a few yards from them. Helpless. Making those little mewing sounds, which nobody had heard. In the days to come, John would think: *All that time I was digging the hideout*, and Connie would think: *When I got to the end of the line there, hanging clothes, I* thought *about checking on her. Why didn't I?*

The guilt would linger. *Those dogs. They were trying to tell us something, and we didn't listen....*

But right now, John would remember, the Hillers were happy.

The storm had passed. The clouds were gone. The rain had only speckled the ground, but it had released all the smells of the dirt, the scent of the pines and firs and cedars above the cutbank. The air was sweet. The beauty of the country – *their* country – came home to them then. It was part of the awe they felt at what had happened to Thelma. It blew over them like a wind, clean and cool; it made their own problems seem trivial, at least for the moment. Wasn't that true?

Yes. That's what John would remember, anyhow.

As the ambulance drove away, its siren wailing, and the rest of the crowd drifted off, the Hillers still stood there. They looked up (as if they had compass needles in their heads; as if they were Indians) and were surprised. Though it had already seemed like night indoors during the storm, and though the lower ridges, sawtoothed with tree-shapes, were dark, the big mountain, Shasta, was still half-lit against a greenish sky. The Hillers breathed in. John could hear them – he could hear himself. Then they breathed out. He thought he glimpsed Hughie's grandmother starting to work her way up through the dimness of her yard, past the blackberry patch, and he edged closer to his parents – staying out of the old witch's sight – just as his father put a hand on his mother's shoulder and said, "I'm sorry, Mouse."

Frank Hiller did say that.

John would swear by it, though by then he was truly feverish. His mother reached out to hug Annie, who had taken off her cowboy hat for dinner but had put it back on. The black brim buckled between them. His father encircled him, John, with an arm so strong, so thick and banded with muscle, that neither Mr. Grissom nor anyone else in the world had a chance of whipping him. Not in the world. They all squeezed together. Sweat, perfume, detergent, chicken, dog poop from somewhere. His father's shoe? John looked down. Then they all looked up again. The lower slopes of Mt. Shasta had turned the color of ashes; the tops of the cones were rose and orange and violet, the glacial ridges knife-edged in shadow. The arrowhead whispered from its shelf. The curved patch of snow still asked its question, and for that moment, at least, John felt he knew the answer. *Were they a family?* Of course they were.

Sump

Sometime in the late 1970s, John Hiller wrote the following.

And decided it was too confused and bitter to be published, and put it in a drawer.

And then, in 2006, after his mother's funeral, he took it out again, partly as a break from writing the thank-you cards she would have written to everyone involved if someone else had died.

She was like that, he thought. Sane and steady and considerate of others to the end. Whatever her faults, she had made his life possible. He knew that now.

As he reread the story – which now seemed to have been written by another person, an angry young man he hardly knew -- John started scribbling notes between the lines, and then longer ones in the margins [like this].

The day the girl I was in love with got married to somebody else, I was down in the sump in back of the Masonic Temple. Imagine a circus cannon with a clown, the would-be projectile, crouched at the bottom. The sump was a hole lined with corrugated pipe, 30 inches in diameter and 15 feet deep, plus the three feet I'd dug down to bedrock. Water trickled between my tennis shoes. An electric pump sucked it out, but sometimes the power failed overnight and I'd come back to find six feet of murk. Draining it again took hours. Even without that, my progress was ridiculously slow. I had to stand in those clown-big shoes on the same ground I was trying to dig up, and what with the pump hose and the dangling light and the ladder and my tools – an Army shovel to scrape the clay and a big crowbar, the kind section gangs used on the Southern Pacific, to break the rock – I could hardly move.

It was August, and hot outside, but down in the sump it was always dim and cool. Sounds filtered in with no sense of direction. When the bells started ringing at the Catholic church down the street, I imagined it was the Methodist church across town where the wedding was going on. Time got mixed up too. It must have been about midday – that's when they hold weddings, after all – but I seem to remember a musty twilight smell and the shadow of Mt. Bradley to the west lying over the hole. A big mountain, pine and fir and man-high manzanita, one I hadn't got around to climbing yet. My home town crouches at the bottom of the Upper Sacramento River canyon, too deep for us ever to see sunsets. All I could see was a circle of pale-blue sky. What the clown sees just before he's blown out into the sickening rush of air and the cheers.

I got ready.

# # # #

"You're cheap labor," my father said – *in a rare tone of apology*, as I remember. "But that's all we can afford." He was master of the lodge that year, and president of the Temple Association. He studied secret ritual in his caboose on trips to Gerber and Klamath Falls, wearing a freight conductor's overalls; then, in tux and apron, he recited it in a fine, strong voice to the lodge's dwindling membership in the Blue Room upstairs from the California Theater. The roof leaked. The carpets were threadbare. Worst of all, the creek that ran underneath the building flooded the theater every winter, sluicing around the seats where, as a kid, I had eater JuJuBes and Sugar Daddies during double bills that cost 50 cents. The operators threatened to leave; they were the temple's only source of income.

"I talked to the city engineer," my father said, "and he says dig the outside sump down another six feet. That should do her." He looked at me. "Shouldn't be too tough for a college grad."

"I – ," I said.

# # # #

I stuttered, you see, even worse then than now. If there isn't much dialogue in this story, it's because I didn't talk much, and I wasn't any better at listening. Rummaging around in my throat for words that got stuck, the way the Sugar Daddies used to stick to my teeth, I hardly heard what other people said. So what dialogue there is here is made up, even more than usual. The strange thing is that the more important it was – the more I still feel myself trembling from it after all those years – the less true it probably is.

For instance, whenever I tell anyone how I was accepted for graduate school at Harvard, I say: *I was already set to go somewhere else, here in California* [UC Davis, in fact], *but I got this letter at the last minute. So I call home and say, 'Hey, Maw, hey, Paw, what do I do?'*

And they say, 'Well, Son, it's your decision and we wouldn't want to influence you in any way – but for God's sake, get your ass off to Harvard before they change their minds.'

So I did.

A comedy routine.

# # # #

At the time, it seemed more like a mistake. A whole series of mistakes. The Army, turning a deaf ear, had awarded me an ROTC commission at the University of Oregon; now it gave me a year off to "pursue further study." As if a master's degree would come in handy when it was time to use one of those entrenching tools in earnest. It was 1966. I hadn't even thought about graduate school until the previous fall, when I found that my professors expected me to go, just as my parents had expected me to go to college in the first place so that I wouldn't have to work on the railroad or in a lumber mill. I was surprised. I'd spent four muffled years in the back rows of their classrooms and believed that, just as the rain outside the windows screened the campus from view, my own diffidence had rendered me invisible. I had no plans, which seemed to surprise *them.* They pointed to my grades. I could have told them that the grades came from doing little else besides read books, but I didn't. I didn't talk to professors at all if I could avoid it. As for Harvard, that year it was trying to recruit students from the backwoods. The Graduate School of Education offered the state of Oregon a couple of fellowships; I filled out a form and happened to win one. Nobody asked how I was supposed to teach when I couldn't talk, any more than the Army had asked how I was supposed to lead men in combat. My parents didn't say anything, and you can be sure I didn't either. It would have seemed ungrateful. We must have known better, but we couldn't help feeling that Harvard had seen "potential" in me, when it had seen only my GPA. We were excited.

We spread out a map on the kitchen table in that long twilight and plotted my route as the sweet air blew in the open window and trains whistled down the canyon. For some reason, I wouldn't receive my fellowship money until I arrived in Cambridge, so I couldn't afford air fare; I had to go by rail. I could travel free on my father's pass as long as I stayed on SP track. He calculated that if I went straight across the country, SP track ended at Salt Lake City; if I detoured south, I could go clear to New Orleans without paying. I don't know if we really gained anything that way. It sounds crazy now. It took six days and five nights, sleeping in my seat. But I didn't ask about that either. The rest of the fare I had to earn, which was why I needed that job.

# # # #

Shouldn't be too tough for a college grad. My father more or less agreed with the Army, which despised intellectuals but had an almost superstitious respect for learning. The books I'd read wouldn't help me dig out the sump, but it was important to dig out the sump so that I could read more books. I went along with this. It would be real work for a change, and so simple, I hoped, that even I couldn't screw it up.

Peter Linz, a lodge buddy of my father's, lent me an old green pickup truck with tools rattling in its bed. A lean, solemn man, he had the only pencil-line mustache in town; his sleeve was pinned up over the stump of his left arm, shot off in a hunting accident. Happily, he didn't ask a lot of questions. As it turned out, I enjoyed getting dirty. I enjoyed shoveling mud into a bucket that my younger sister, Annie, hauled up on a pulley fixed to the back porch of the temple. I even enjoyed getting blisters from pounding that crowbar on the rock. Lava or granite: our mountainsides had both. I pounded the steel point of that sucker flat. The rock didn't budge.

# # # #

One midnight soon after I started, the phone rang. I woke up enough to hear my mother say, "Well, gee, I don't know. Frank's out on the road. I mean the railroad. He won't be back till tomorrow." Her voice was sleepy, but I heard a certain tone in it. I didn't hear words so well, but I did hear tones of voice sometimes. This was the cautious, grudging tone she used when she'd already decided to do someone a kindness but didn't want to admit it, aware that kindness always runs a risk. A floorboard in the hall creaked under her weight. "Well, I guess so," she said finally. "Just stay put." Then she chuckled. "I guess you poor kids can't do anything else."

In the morning we had two guests for breakfast. About my age. But older, of course. A blonde *who stretched and yawned like a cat* and whose suntanned arms, in the light through the kitchen window and the big Douglas fir across the street, showed tiny golden hairs. A husky guy in a T-shirt whose face, in the same light, looked pasty. He had pimples, and pouches under his eyes. It was his car, apparently, that had thrown a rod south of town. A highway patrolman had brought them in, and the girl, whose father belonged to the same fly-casting club as Uncle George, my mother's brother in San Francisco, had remembered these *people* she was supposed to call if anything happened on the way to Portland ... this *phone number* she had in her address book somewhere ... and there it was. "We're really, really grateful," she said. "I mean, like total strangers calling you up in the middle of the night."

Maybe she didn't say that exactly. KWSD Radio in Mount Shasta City may have been playing a polka [almost the only kind of music that station played]; I may have been watching a squirrel run from the fir to the black oak in our yard and hoping it would charm her. The words sound hippieish, and the hippies hadn't appeared yet. But again I remember the tone. She was polite, she was sincere, but she wasn't really apologizing. She seemed to feel that she had a right to be there, or anywhere else circumstance happened to put her. Her voice could convey all this at once. That shocked me.

# # # #

Once, when I was visiting Annie in Sacramento, where she worked as a Capitol lobbyist for the regional Building Industry Association, I asked her if she remembered Karin Bernstein.

"Oh, yeah," she said. "Definitely. She was a big deal, for me, anyway." I must have looked surprised. "Oh, sure. The *clothes* she had. All real casual, you know, sportswear and stuff, but expensive. You could tell. *I* could, anyway. A city girl. I learned a lot from her when she was there. I think she had fun showing me – the country mouse didn't know from nothin' in those days. Like when she took that fall out of her hair the first time, I darn near fell over."

"What fall?"

"In her hair. It was fake, but it matched the rest of her hair just perfectly."

"I'll be damned," I said.

"You mean you didn't notice?"

"She had a wig?"

"No, no. Just this bunch of hair that she pinned in there. The same streaky blonde." She was amused. "You mean, with all that staring you did – "

"I noticed that bathing suit," I said.

# # # #

My mother said they could stay as long as it took to get the car fixed. The Commercial Garage had to send for parts. It might be a week, even two. From that first breakfast on, I think, we all conspired. We took them to the town swimming pool and up to Castle Lake and ate fried chicken at the picnic table out back while the yellowjackets buzzed us. My parents wouldn't let them share a room, of course, so my sister and I had to spread sleeping bags on the grass. We didn't mind. We wanted Karin and Ned – that was the boyfriend's name – to believe that we were simpler and warmer and more hospitable than city folks. They seemed to want to believe that too. It all went fine.

# # # #

My memory of leaving, though, is all wrong. The train that would eventually get me to Harvard stopped in Dunsmuir at 2 a.m., but I remember *sunlight and frost on the rails and steam hissing around the great flanged wheels*. There wouldn't have been frost in September; that came from riding the "milk train" to Eugene the last four Christmases and Easters. The steam came from even earlier, when I was a little boy and the SP hadn't yet switched to diesel. I falsely remember the train pulling out under the black-painted wooden footbridge that arched from the station to the engine shops and roundhouse, both gone now. In 1960, kids were let out of high school to stand on that bridge and hear John F. Kennedy speak during the last of the whistle-stop campaigns. [If we'd known then what we know now about Kennedy's womanizing, would we have let a girl from my school, Sandra Smith, the newly crowned Miss Siskiyou, in *her* bathing suit, which left little to the imagination, hand him a jug of Dunsmuir water, touted the Best on Earth? It was a more innocent time altogether.] We looked almost straight down on his reddish-brown head. The Secret Service didn't seem to care.

So all my real leaving is forgotten, lost for good. Except for one memory, which is true even though it, too, is borrowed from those earlier trips to college. I didn't want to leave. Lord knows, I should have wanted to; every country boy I've ever heard of, real or fictional, has wanted to; but I didn't. I wanted to stay.

# # # #

"You dropped a bucket on me," I told my sister on that same visit. "Do you remember that?"

She said she didn't.

"I do. A full, loaded bucket. Right between the shoulder blades. Down in that hole, I didn't have any room to duck."

"You sure? It wasn't on purpose."

"I didn't say it was. I'm just saying it really hit me. *Bang.* Knocked my breath out."

"Probably served you right," she said. "Even if I did. The way you picked on me. All those years of throwing snowballs at me in the winter, acorns in the fall, those pointy grass things in the summer. Foxtails. You had it coming."

She was right, of course. I'd been a shameless pest of an older brother, teasing her unmercifully until, as I knew she would sooner or later, she'd blow up. Once she kicked me in the shin with a steel-tipped ski boot. But that bucket of mud was really the last of our atrocities. That summer she wasn't a kid anymore. Everything seemed about to change.

Now, sitting with her legs crossed yoga-style on her sofa in the little house on 42nd Street that she'd kept after her divorce, a calico cat on either side of her, Annie looked at me. Her animation faded. I knew what she was thinking. It's what she must have thought whenever she saw me in those days, when it seemed as if I'd never hold a job for long, never get married at all. She was wondering whether I'd ever get my ass in gear. But she must have decided that it didn't do any good to say so.

All she said was: "What's all this instant replay for, anyway? I mean not so instant. It's all *old.*"

# # # #

Whenever I tell this story....

[I kept writing that, but when *did* I tell this story, except on paper, here, and then to myself, over and over?]

...I say: *Somehow I knew, right from the first, that Ned was on the way out. She was going to dump him eventually.* But maybe I say this just because I found out years later that they did split up; at the time, maybe, all I noticed was that Karin seemed more comfortable in her tawny skin than he did in his. He had those pimples. He burned in the sun. His face wore a squint that didn't go away. He couldn't stop worrying about his car and what it was going to cost him.

Not to mention all the time he was losing, the time he could have spent alone with her. No, I still see his vulnerability as sexual. But right now, for the first time, the weirdest thought comes to me: *Did my father like her too?* I mean, he wasn't so impossibly old, when I come to think of it. Did he scope her out on the sly? It makes sense, even though I can't believe it, not really. Not about him. [It was only in my slanderous, resentful imagination -- a truer portrait of me than of him -- that he once might have lusted after dusky, unattainable señoritas.] Still, he gazed at her mildly, watching TV after dinner with a can of Olympia beer on the arm of his chair; he didn't seem to grumble as much as he usually did about how sitcom husbands were made to look like a bunch of nincompoops. He talked head gaskets and manifolds with Ned, perhaps glad to find someone my age who cared about such things. He certainly never raised a fuss about their being there.

But how did Karin see *him*? That concerned me more. It came to me slowly that I hadn't looked my father full in the face in years.

Not that I started looking at him then, but I watched her look and tried to imagine what she saw, and I realized that to her he was ordinary. That, too, was shocking. She had no fear of him, any more than my mother seemed to. About my sister I wasn't sure. She felt it in a different way, I believed. At any rate, she was nothing like Karin, who would curl up in her chair with her smooth legs tucked under her and *her eyes shining with what seemed to be the sheer joy of argument*, challenging him to justify the Brotherhood of Railroad Trainmen's opposition to an SP plan to eliminate firemen in diesel locomotives. Why pay a coal-shoveler when there was no coal to shovel? My father quoted the union gospel, which had always been gospel to me, too:

"It's a safety factor. You need a pair of eyes on both sides of the train. Otherwise God knows what'll happen. Hotboxes, fires, you name it. These crewcuts" – his name for the railroad's new breed of college-trained efficiency experts – "try to tell me, who runs the damn trains, who's run 'em for twenty years, that we don't need an extra man. Well, I say we do." *And he would smack the arm of his chair with his fist.*

But Karin would just tilt her head and smile a little and say, "Sounds like featherbedding to me."

I think I remember this – but what about his can of beer? Did he finish it before he hit the chair, or did he hold it up with his other hand? And then I wonder if I didn't make that part up.

[Oh, he hit the chair, all right, more than once, in my sight. But as I wrote this I was thinking more of what my mother told me after he'd died in 1975, of liver failure, at fifty-nine. He'd been ailing for several years – a gall-bladder operation, part of his large intestine removed, a colostomy bag. Those railroad hours had finally worn him down. He couldn't hunt or fish anymore. So he drank. The can of Oly became a fifth of Jim Beam. The SP caught him drinking on the job and fired him just short of minimum retirement age, after thirty-seven years with the company, and then, in shame, he settled into that chair and drank himself to death. It took about six months. His skin turned a jaundiced yellow. "He said terrible things to me," my mother said. "Mean things. He said if he had it to do over again, he wouldn't have married me.... But of course he wasn't himself by then. Not the Frank I knew."

[Stoic as ever, she watched him go down and didn't tell Annie or me. And I had put all the distance between us I could. The first I knew, he was already dead. When I got the call to go to his funeral, I was visiting a Vietnam War buddy in Texas.]

# # # #

"He was waiting for you to fight," my mother said more than once. "Don't you understand? He wanted you to rebel. Oh, he might have growled some, but he would have respected you if you'd talked back to him. Don't you see?"

I wanted to believe her, but I couldn't, quite. It sounded too much like something in the books my father and I agreed weren't real. And not very good books at that. Sometimes, as a kid, I'd thought my mother really didn't know how frightened I was. Even after that talk, I wasn't sure she had. She must have felt that *parents should stand together* – she said that sometimes – or that too much sympathy would spoil me, or very possibly that it might spoil her. I could ask her, maybe, but it seems pointless now....

[Never mind *now*. Good God.]

Notes weren't enough, John decided. A thorough rethinking was needed. In his home office in L.A. – just a corner of his bedroom -- he yawned and leaned back in his swivel chair from the manuscript and the pile of thank-you cards he'd set aside for it. He had driven north for the funeral with his wife and his college-age son. He had sat at the same kitchen table, in front of the same window, looking out at the same Douglas fir, the same oak, descendants of the same gray squirrels, that he and his parents had seen when they planned his trip to Boston forty years before. Only this time it had been January – snow banked beside the streets, black slick on the pavement. A boy, ten or eleven years old

– John didn't know the kid, didn't know a lot of people in Dunsmuir now – turned the corner from Needham Avenue, wearing only a flannel shirt and a maroon knit cap. No mittens. He scooped up handfuls of snow and fired them at trees and telephone poles. Something about the random, bored, almost angry way he did this reminded John of his former self. He had thrown snowballs at the same trees, the same poles. He could feel the pain in the kid's bare hands as he squeezed slush into ice.

What had happened to *him*? The boy he had been?

He had written the sump story to explain to himself what had happened. It had taken him years – an embarrassingly long time – to arrive at a basic insight: He was damaged. His father, probably, had broken his spirit (though without meaning to). He had carried that damage with him even after he thought he'd left his father far behind, climbed out of the canyon and the hole at the bottom of it.

Insight is victory, and hard won. It feels good, which is why he could write so coldly about his parents here – especially his mother – and so pessimistically about his own future. But this insight was a crude one -- almost as inadequate as the ways he'd previously described his life to himself (in italics): *A comedy routine.*

Too many things didn't fit. *What about the Bear River Grade, for Pete's sake?* John asked himself now.

[The Bear River runs through the Sierra Nevada foothills between Colfax and Auburn. Dad's friend Bud Jones, having taken early retirement from the Aerojet plant in Sacramento, had bought a little ranch out there. Just twenty-five acres. A tumbledown house, a barn, a pasture and a pear orchard. He and his family were harvesting the pears when we visited in September of 1965. Bud had broken his arm falling out of a tree. My father didn't want to drive. Our car had boiled over pulling the trailer. Steam from the radiator had scalded him when he bent over to unscrew the cap. Just the touch of the wheel on his stomach was agony. But neither my mother nor I could tow the trailer to his satisfaction, so he'd driven the rest of the way himself, in simmering silence. That was all the driving he was going to do, he let us know when we arrived. And a damn sight more than he should have had to.

The women shied away from Bud's old stakebed truck with its balky stick shift. So it fell to me to drive the pears to market. Bud rode beside me and offered what advice he could. The two-lane road switchbacked down through heat-struck grass and oaks and jack pines to the river, then steeply back up. A single missed shift could have been disaster. The brakes were too worn to stop the truck if it ever got going downhill too fast; the engine was too feeble to pull us up the grade unless I kept the revs high. It didn't take much imagination to see us overturned and crates of pears scattered everywhere. It was a much sterner test than I'd just failed with Dad and the trailer, but Bud's calming presence made all the difference. I did it *perfectly.*

[Dad looked skeptical when Bud told him what a fine job I'd done, but I knew. I was all right after all.

[Wasn't I?]

John, still remembering how he'd sat at his mother's kitchen table, watching the kid outside, thought about crossing out paragraphs wholesale, changing the entire story to fit how he saw things now, but at last decided not to. The angry, lonely young man who wrote it had existed too. He ought to have his say.

# # # #

No, Karin didn't take away the fear, but she made me more aware of it. Aware enough to want to hide it. For so long it had been so central a fact that I'd stopped even looking for reasons. Just by being there, she seemed to say that I should be looking, that the fear was a habit I should have outgrown. The previous summer [before Bear River] I'd gone through the ROTC's version of basic training at Fort Lewis, Wash., and something had happened there, too. Between push-ups and running and getting yelled at, skirmishing through the fir forests below Mt. Rainier and sleeping on anthills, scraping paint off the barracks windows with a razor blade and blasting away on the firing ranges with the old M-1s we trained with, something else had happened that seemed to indicate that I wasn't a victim, as I liked to think, but something worse. This didn't come to me all at once, but Karin started it. The sump did the rest.

####

At first the job seemed a kind of haven. It was my father's idea, after all. I wore clown's motley – old jeans and cords, short-sleeved button-down shirts that had never been fashionable – but that was excused. I didn't own a car, but I had Peter Linz's truck. If I didn't speak, I could act nobly exhausted. I imagined myself as John Wayne climbing off his horse and striding the dusty main street of a new town while saloon girls and schoolmarms alike peeked through the windows; I hoped Karin would find my silence a challenge and finally a source of interest. This hadn't ever worked before, but it was the only plan I had.

####

Before long, though, my safety eroded. I had to admit to myself that the job wasn't going well.

As the days dragged by, my initial confidence gave way to frustration, then to a creeping panic: a sequence that always seemed new to me until some moment when I realized I knew it by heart. Just digging the first yard of clay and gravel seemed to take forever. The pump kept quitting and re-flooding the hole. Then I hit the rock. I wore out the crowbar; there was no room to swing a pick. I risked electrocution by trying to riddle the rock with a power drill, but the drill bits were too small to penetrate it and got stuck or broke off. Finally my sister left. There was nothing for her to haul on the pulley anymore.

Around then, at breakfast, the subject of my ROTC deferment came up, and Karin asked, "What do you think about the war?"

"N-not much," I managed to say.

"Good," she said. "I don't think any intelligent person, any *decent* person, could be for it."

Or something like that. I don't remember any hippie tone here. Still, her gray-green eyes had the authority of the Bay Area behind them. I didn't ask how she could be so sure. Instead, I thought of the students down there who were demonstrating, burning their draft cards, fleeing to Canada – all the uproar that had echoed dimly even in Eugene. How stupid of me to imagine that physical work would impress her. She wanted courage, especially of the moral kind. She wanted to know how anybody smart enough to go to Harvard could have joined the Army in the first place. And I couldn't tell her. I didn't know myself. During those days alone in the sump, I felt other thoughts rise to the surface, thoughts that seemed to have waited a long time to be born in the darkness, the trickle of water and the hollow pinging of the pipe: about why I was so much younger than I should have been, how even the decisions other people hadn't made for me were still not my own. I didn't want to think about any of this. It was bad enough that I had to do what I'd sworn never to do when I took the job – ask my father for help.

# # # #

South of Bakersfield, the grass gave out. This is probably wrong too. I must be remembering some later trip by car; any passenger train would have gone down the coast to L.A. But it doesn't matter much. The rail lines rejoined at Barstow, in the middle of the Mojave. To my eyes, the Central Valley, with its yellow grass rippling in the heat, was desert enough. South of Bakersfield, even the grass gave out into a land of scattered brush and naked rock, into an emptiness I'd never seen before.

# # # #

My father's eyes narrowed. He was unhappy, and about more than broken drill bits. But he held his temper. I guess he figured he had no choice. He went to City Hall again and borrowed a jackhammer and an air compressor. "Make it quick," he said. "The racket this damn thing makes, first thing you know the neighbors'll be up in arms. They'll blame the city, and that'll get us in dutch."

The compressor looked like an automobile engine mounted on wheels, like the front end of a tractor. We parked it in the gutter and attached the air hose to the jackhammer, which also could be used as a drill. The bit that came with it was an inch and a half in diameter and four feet long. Plenty big enough, we thought.

After he left, I gripped the heavy tool one-handed, looped the hose over my shoulder and worked my way slowly down the ladder. Outside, the compressor idled. I braced one foot on the last rung and the other on a stub of drain pipe, poked the bit into the ground and squeezed the handles. The noise was deafening. The light swung wildly and the vibration banged me against the corrugated wall and a hurricane of mud spattered me from head to toe.

# # # #

What a hillbilly I was! I was in high school and reading Leon Uris' novel "Exodus" before it dawned on me that there were Jews in the modern world, not just in biblical times. I'd known about the Nazis, of course – from Mrs. Ordoñez in our old neighborhood, on Shasta Avenue – but somehow not about the Jews. For some reason, this embarrassed me more than bad things I'd done on purpose. At Oregon I tried to make up for it by reading Saul Bellow and Bernard Malamud and "The Rise and Fall of the Third Reich." But the shame didn't go away. A mistake like that didn't seem to be one I *could* make up for, any more than the world could make up for turning its back while millions went to their deaths. I was part of the world. I had turned by back, even if I hadn't meant to. But had I somehow meant to without knowing it? I wondered what Karin Bernstein would think, though I didn't dare ask. Not that I knew for sure that she was Jewish. There was just the name. Yet, because of her, I started brooding about it again down in the sump. She seemed to touch all my secrets. True, there hadn't been any

Jews in Dunsmuir, that I knew of. Once or twice my father had talked about somebody "Jewing down" somebody else in a business deal, but that hadn't even sounded like prejudice; it was just a phrase. Still, for a hotshot student like me, what could excuse such ignorance?

Worse than ignorance.

Searching the past for clues I might have overlooked, I remembered a comic book. Not one of the Dells or Disneys, with their seals of approval, I was allowed to read at home, but a horror comic I'd borrowed from a friend in the seventh grade. Ragged people were starving to death in a Nazi concentration camp. Of course. *They must have been Jews.* On their last legs, they made a man out of mud from the floor of their barracks. Called a golem. They prayed for revenge. Then they died. When the guards came, the mud-man stirred, seized the shovel that had created him and cracked the Nazis' skulls. Bullets just went through him. When other guards came, they found nothing – just their comrades' corpses under a pile of earth like a grave.

I liked that. Wearing my oldest clothes, smeared with mud, I looked like a golem as much as a clown. I tried to feel like one, too, as I climbed out of the hole each afternoon. An instrument of vengeance, bent on destruction. I slouched. I squished. *I scared little kids*, I always say. My tennis shoes leaked brown slime on the sidewalk.

At the Commercial Garage, where work on Ned's car seemed equally paralyzed, I slapped him on his white-T-shirted shoulder and enjoyed seeing him flinch. Then back uptown, past the theater to Gibson's Union 76 station, where I'd parked the truck. By then the mud had dried; I could brush some of it off. I drove home. Over the Sacramento River bridge. Slowing at the swimming pool, next to the ball park. Even stopping, with a heavy stare and my filthy arm on the hot metal of the door, if Karin was there.

I noticed that bathing suit. Oh, yes. It was more than a two-piece, and Dunsmuir had seen few enough of those [Sandra Smith's being one of them]. It was a black bikini with fine black fishnet between top and bottom. The hollow of her navel, the curve of her slender waist, seemed all the sexier for being half veiled. *She got attention*, I always say. From local guys I couldn't compete with, though they couldn't even compete with Ned. They hot-dogged around the diving board. Whooped and splashed. She leaned back against the chain-link fence, ignoring them. She always kept her hair dry, but I could see drops of water glistening on her back. That perfect skin. The wire of the fence made a pattern on it. Behind her, the blue-green surface of the pool wove nets of light. I was close enough to smell chlorine and tanning oil. Once she turned, her eyes big in her triangular face, and saw me in the truck. She waved. (Take that, you bastards.) And smiled.

I waved back.

# # # #

By now you must be wondering: What about the girl I said I was in love with – the one who was going to get married?

I wondered too, because down in the sump, among all the other uneasy thoughts, one more lay coiled like a rattler: the thought that, as much as I loved her, I knew almost nothing about her. She had moved to Dunsmuir during my senior year in high school. [Actually, she was a foreign exchange student. Say she was French, which she wasn't, and that her name was Gabrielle, ditto. She had left after her year here but returned to the States for college.] And maybe that was the whole point to her attractiveness, like Karin's – her newness, when most of the other girls I'd known since kindergarten. If I were telling *that* story, I could describe her down to the last mole and gesture, but I'm not. Let's just say that *the first time I saw her, in the school's opening-day assembly in September of 1961, her smile lit up the gym.*

The second time was at a Methodist church camp. I was in the midst of one of my flirtations with religion – a recurring wistfulness that could never quite overcome my conviction that churches, all churches, were based on fear, just as much as the Army. Mostly I went to see her. The camp was up in the mountains near Castle Lake. Even this early in the fall, it was so cold at that elevation that the boys, who slept outside on the ground, half froze. The girls slept in a log cabin with a fireplace. At dawn, I struggled out of my sleeping bag fully dressed. I stretched and shivered. Sunlight splintered through the pines. I took deep breaths of the air, of what suddenly seemed to be pure exultation. I could hear voices and smell bacon and woodsmoke from the cabin, and I started walking there in a kind of trance. I was going to be near her, and for a short time, because she was new, she wouldn't know I wasn't supposed to be; as long as I didn't open my mouth, I would be OK.

And that's it, really. That's the beginning and, in a sense, the end, too. Gabrielle figured things out soon enough, though she was friendly and never outright discouraged me; we talked now and then, about school stuff, but there was never any *dialogue*. I thought I wanted some. I planned it months in advance, sometimes – how I was going to ask her out or simply tell her I loved her. The unspoken words in my mind grew deeper and heavier, like winter snowpack, until I was weighed down by conflicting anxieties: that the pent-up avalanche would shock and repel her, and that it would dribble out like meltwater with no effect at all. So when the time came I didn't say the words, or I said them only obliquely. That left me hope.

Maybe only a country boy and a stutterer can imagine that he has so much time, that the rest of the world is going to wait for him. I went to Oregon [where I took three years of French so that I could write her letters – not that I could ever speak the language] and she went to UC Berkeley. She gave me an excuse not to take the girls I met at college too seriously, not to risk too much. [So I was dateless there as well.] Sometimes she answered my letters and praised my halting French. I still had hope. More than that: I had confidence that someday the words would be spoken, if necessary in spite of me. She has to know, I thought. She *does* know. I shouldn't have to say anything..

Once during those years, my mother said: "I'll have to hand it to you. You must have a real feeling for this girl."

Strangely, that made me doubt it for the first time.

And strangely, too, now that Gabrielle was marrying an aspiring orthopedic surgeon she'd met down at Cal, the only consolation was that she hadn't invited me to the wedding. This couldn't be an oversight, I thought. She must have felt that avalanche trembling over her head. As much as she'd tried to hide it, she knew.

Didn't she?

But, as I say, my own feeling was in question now. If a chance remark from my mother could do it, having Karin around only made things worse. My love seemed like the Egyptian mummies I'd read about as a kid, which could stay intact for centuries when sealed in their tombs but disintegrated at the first touch of air. I didn't tell Karin about it, of course, but I knew what she would say ... thought I knew, from the way she said other things.

# # # #

Finally I couldn't stand it any longer. One afternoon when my father was gone, I played hooky from the job and drove Peter Linz's truck up the Castle Lake road. It surprised me that I remembered so well where the twin ruts turned off. I bumped through a dry ford that had been a creek that fall, and saw the cabin. It stood more alone in a clearing than I remembered. The camp was empty. I got out. Insects chanted in the dry grass. Ths scrape of my footsteps on stones sounded unnaturally loud. I tried to find the place where I'd slept in the trees; then I followed my own trail from there to the cabin door. I think I was trying to disillusion myself, to kill *teen-age romanticism* for good. Instead, strangest of all, what I almost hadn't dared hope for happened: I fell into that same trance, as if all the time in between had been erased.

No breakfast smells this time, but another, indefinable smell that stung in my nostrils like rotting leaves. The smell of memory. The door was covered with cedar bark, brown and gray and purple. In the sun's glare, the purple seemed to pulse like the blood in my eyes. I stood there, hypnotized by it – that, and the gray dirt and twigs at the entrance. Old footprints. Mine? Hers? I wasn't thinking straight anymore. I nearly fainted; it was like being slugged in the stomach. So much pain, and so much happiness that I could feel it still. At that moment, though this didn't turn out to be true, I thought it would last me forever.

# # # #

What did last was the rock. By the time Karin and Ned left, it was drilled through and through like Swiss cheese, but it didn't split or crumble; I couldn't pry loose more then chips. By then it seemed more than a boulder. It seemed to be the core of the entire earth.

A kind of daze set in. Every morning, if the pump had failed, I drained the hole; if not, I climbed down and used the jackhammer and got coated with mud. I no longer expected to finish the job. I couldn't believe how long it had taken, and I couldn't expect anyone else to believe it, especially my father. But though I'd secretly given up, I kept on working. I didn't dare quit. I just hoped that sooner or later he would see that it was hopeless and call a halt. He didn't. I had no more strength, but I leaned limply against the job with all my weight, and he kept propping it up.

It was like ROTC boot camp. And how I'd managed to get through that was my last and deepest secret.

The Army, turning a deaf ear: Not true. It wasn't their fault. I fooled them. They may have been about to wash me out – I felt they were – but by then I was so miserable that I didn't care anymore, and it was exactly because I didn't care, even a little bit, that I stopped stuttering. Totally. For two whole weeks. I barked out orders in the "command voice" they wanted us all to develop, as if their system had worked on me and I'd had a sudden infusion of confidence. When all I'd really gained was the bittersweet knowledge that my stuttering wasn't a physical affliction, as I'd always thought. It was a defect in character....

[And yet. It *is* physical, researchers today apparently agree. Glitchy wiring in the brain, with a genetic component. My brother, Tommy, whose character is unimpeachable, also stutters. Since those two weeks at Fort Lewis, I've had other more or less brief intervals of fluency, but the stuttering always returns, and I've learned to stop blaming myself so harshly when it does. This, though, was the first time, and my disappointment was profound.]

...No wonder I could forget the Jews. *You'd forget your head if it wasn't screwed on*, my father used to say. They named me the Most Improved in my trainee platoon. And sure enough: Once I started to believe them, started to care again, started to hope that the cure would be permanent, the stuttering came back.

Now my mother said, "He's proud of you for sticking at it for so long."

But when I finally told him ... what I remember is how the compressor popped in the silence, how his face half turned away and how the side of his weathered neck was creased and veined and mottled like stone. *Lava or granite.* Now his shoulders under the overall straps were slightly stooped but as massive as ever. I felt disgust coming off him in waves, like the smell of sweat, but heavy, like the rock: a whole mountainside of disgust that squeezed the breath out of me and made me realize that nothing between us had changed since I was five.

"Tony Sirianni," he said at last. Not to me. "He's the SP's powder monkey. Maybe *he* can do something."

# # # #

He was waiting for you to fight, but even if he was, how could I fight if I was always in the wrong, unless I was too angry to care?

[Oh, I did, once, sort of – the last Christmas before I went to Vietnam. That was a year and a half after the sump job. You might say it was a dispute over film criticism. We were watching "The Bridge on the River Kwai" on TV, and Dad remarked that they didn't make 'em anymore like the British Col. Nicholson, the Alec Guinness character, who would rather roast in a tiny punishment cell of sheet iron – tighter than the pipe behind the Masonic Temple – than give in to his Japanese captors. "There's a man with guts, who stands up for his principles," Dad said – never mind that the principle in this case was that officers shouldn't do manual labor. And I told him – smart-ass college boy – that the movie was *ambiguous;* that Nicholson was supposed to be a hero, yes, but a madman too.

[You wouldn't think that would matter, but remember, this was the Sixties. Dad had praised the colonel for a reason, and I had – though without consciously intending to – thrown his argument back in his face, and he understood perfectly. "These ideas!" he cried, glancing around at Mom, Annie, the dog that followed Cleo, the tinseled tree, the front door shingled with Christmas cards, for support. "Where the hell does he get these *ideas*?"

[Then he threatened to knock me through a wall. And though he was aging and sick by then, I never doubted that he could.

["He's afraid you'll get yourself killed," my mother said as soon as she could get me alone, "He's afraid you'll hesitate, you'll *think* too much, instead of shoot."

[I didn't argue. But I thought: Is this *respect?* To still be treated like a kid when I was twenty-two years old, a lieutenant in the United States Army, a graduate of the Artillery and Missile School at Fort Sill, Okla., where I'd learned to "adjust" the fire of real shells from real cannons?

[Probably my mistake was to imagine that if I finally fought him, all his resistance would melt away. Instead of its being, in fact, a *fight*.

["He loves you," my mother said. "You should know that by now. He doesn't know how to say it, I know. But he shouldn't have to anymore."]

I never seemed to get angry back then, or almost never. I'd start to sometimes, but then it would dwindle away. In all that summer, I remember only one time.

That was when the train stopped in El Paso, after a thousand miles of desert. A soldier and his bride got on. They sat down in the seat opposite me and watched the mesquite-dotted plains slide by. This much I remember for sure. At least I think it was mesquite. The soldier said he'd just been discharged, but he still wore his uniform; as a future officer in disguise, I noticed his Pfc. stripe. He looked – what can I say? He looked normal. Big hands and a big Adam's apple, a forehead sunburned below where his helmet liner had been. She looked retarded. Pale hair and white skin, like an albino's, except that albinos have pink eyes. Hers were blue. Her mouth hung open. Her dress was blue too, frilly and flimsy. They seemed to be honeymooners; she wiggled onto his lap – for my benefit, I think – and cuddled and kissed him, arms around his neck.

So I said, 'How long you folks been married?'

And he said, or she said, I'm not sure, 'Three days."

And I said, 'Well, congratulations,' and they looked at each other, mighty pleased with themselves.

Then I said – it's the funniest thing. I remember asking this, but I don't remember what led up to it. I said, 'How long did you know each other before you decided to get hitched?'

And he said, 'Five hours.'

Can you believe it? That's a record, as far as I'm concerned.

More comedy. The strangest thing to me now is that I believed him absolutely, never questioned him. I gathered that as soon as they'd decided to get married, they'd done it. Is that possible, even in Las Vegas? Or Mexico? I have no idea. I didn't ask for details. I *wanted* to believe him, because that was the moment when I was really pissed. And the girl sensed it. Maybe because she *was* retarded, she had an instinct. Her face went all wrong angles, and she shrank against him. She started to cry.

"Hey, what's the matter?' the soldier asked. Then he looked at me. "You got a problem, buddy?"

I spread my hands and rolled my eyes.

"She don't want you staring at her," he said. "She don't like people who stare."

"I w-wasn't staring," I said.

They didn't leave then, but the next time I went to the men's room and came back they were gone. *Before they got off in Houston,* I always say, *they'd already started snapping at each other.* Which is true. I overheard them. But what I don't say is that I had no pity for the girl [which is doubly shameful because of my brother], although I could imagine a cruel future for her – for both of them, actually. I was furious. Even if it made no sense. I didn't want her, I tried to tell myself, but she'd done for this bozo what, I was sure, neither she nor anyone else would do for me.

# # # #

Sometimes I tell it differently. The last Sunday before Karin and Ned left, we played golf. I drove them over the eastern ridge to McCloud, where the lumber company had a nine-hole course.

"He's pretty good," she warned me. "He used to be on the golf team in high school."

I was rusty, and my blistered hands were sore, but as I say in this version, *I didn't sweat it.* Ned's mind was still on his car. And McCloud was a course that gave outsiders fits. The greens were tiny and lumpy and slow, spotted with snow mold left over from winter. *I took it all out on him*, I say. *All my frustration. Poor guy. I really bore down and murdered him.*

Trouble is, I don't think it happened that way. I was having too good a time, in the open air, on holiday from the job. I don't think I even cared that much about impressing Karin. When Ned started squinting and cussing, she took his hand as they walked down the fairways, as close as they'd been since they came. That should have made me feel bad enough to remember, but I don't.

What I do remember is riding back, squeezed together in Peter Linz's truck. We passed Snowman's Hill summit and started down. On the right was Mt. Shasta -- double-coned, patched with snow even in August, fourteen thousand feet high, the center of all that country; even today, in L.A., you could put me in a dark room and spin me around and I could sense its direction. At least I like to think so. Ahead was the slope falling miles to the river, and then more mountains. Eddy and Bradley and Castle Crags. The greens of the forest, and the sky about an hour from sunset. You could see sunsets up here. The truck chugged along; it couldn't do much more than 50. Karin's thigh brushed against mine. *The only time I touched her*, I say, though that's probably just a lie like the rest.

# # # #

I got ready.

My return to the church camp had convinced me. I'd been a coward. I'd had a real feeling and denied it, called it *teen-age romanticism*, buried it in the ground like the wasted talent in the Bible, and the wedding was my punishment. I didn't deserve the girl I loved. But the feeling wasn't about to disappear just because she married somebody else. It would go on and on. Down in the sump, I listened to the bells. I savored the pain, felt it swell inside me, as achingly rich as the harmony in certain doo-wop songs; it seemed strong enough for anything.

Then I knew. The only way to prove that I loved Gabrielle was to do something radical. Even if it was too late. And I knew what to do. When I finished work, I'd collect the tools and take the truck home; then I'd cross the river on George West's footbridge and head up Mt. Bradley with just the clothes I had on. Climb it at last. And then keep walking, night and day. There was nothing between me and the Pacific Ocean but mountains, a hundred miles of them. The Trinity Alps. The Marble Mountain Wilderness. Forks of Salmon. I wouldn't get even half that far before I'd drop. Crawl under a bush like an animal to die.

But she'd know.

And so would everybody else.

# # # #

Powder monkey fit Tony Sirianni. He was a little man with an agile, crouching way of walking and long, hairy arms. He brought some of the SP's dynamite. My father had gone to City Hall again; this time, I think, some political pull was involved. Tony Sirianni studied the back wall of the temple. "No good," he said. "She's loose, loose brick there. Put too much in and *blooie*, she all come down, all over the street. No good."

I didn't say anything. It wasn't really my responsibility anymore.

He looked down the sump and muttered some more about how the wall was too close to it, but I guess he wanted to try anyway. He dropped half a stick of dynamite into one of the deepest holes I'd drilled. He tamped mud and gravel on top of it and ran the fuse outside. Then we piled old quilts and doormats on top of that. When he set it off, we were standing across the street in the sun.

The explosion wasn't very loud, but the ground shook. The wall held. A little smoke appeared under the porch.

There! I remember thinking. *If that doesn't do it, nothing will.*

I ran up to the sump, and he pulled me away. "Wait, you crazy? You breathe that stuff, you get sick. Or die, and then what do I tell your papa? Just wait."

He got a rake, and we fished out the quilts and mats. He was right. Just a few whiffs of the acrid fumes made me woozy. We waited another half-hour.

Then he climbed down and looked, and found that despite the tamping, the force of the dynamite had shot straight up out of the hole, like a shell out of a cannon, without cracking the rock at all.

"What now?" I asked.

Tony Sirianni started loading the quilts into his truck.

"Aren't --. I mean, aren't you going to t-try—." I got stuck. Swallowed. Licked my lips. "A whole stick?"

"Hell, no," he said. "I learn a long time ago in *this* business, you don't press your luck. A whole stick." He looked at the temple wall again, shook his head and grinned. "No way. You tell your papa. I'm sorry, but it's just no good."

So that was it. As far as I know [and I drove past the temple just after my mother's funeral], the rock is there to this day.

# # # #

I spent six weeks down in the sump. The Temple Association paid me $200. It paid my sister too. Before I left for the East, both my father and my mother found a chance to talk to me alone.

After we dropped off the truck at Peter Linz's, my father walked beside me to his car with his hands in his pockets and his head hunched down into his shoulders. He didn't quite look at me. I knew that Masons were required to believe in God, but my father had never spoken to me about religion. I thought he was going to say something else. About the accident, maybe. Or about failure in general. I stiffened. But this turned out to be one of those moments I remember when he didn't seem disgusted with me so much as simply puzzled. I was such an odd kid. I never answered back. Maybe, like the Army, he didn't know what else to do with me.

Anyway, he cleared his throat. Then he said that just because he didn't go to church, it didn't mean that he didn't think there had to be some kind of Higher Power. He said the universe was a damn sight too big and complicated to run itself. Even at Harvard, he said, they wouldn't be able to argue with that. Then he patted my shoulder and urged me, wherever I went, to keep the faith.

This startled me so much that I told my mother about it. She did look at me – a long, level look. She shook her head. "It's just too bad," she said. "Too bad you two had to be born so different, have such different personalities. That's all it is."

I grunted.

It must have sounded sullen, because all at once she blazed up at me, in a tone of voice I've heard her use only two or three times in my life. "You had a *wonderful* childhood," she said. "In country like this. Don't you ever forget it."

And it seemed at that moment that I had, if I'd only been able to catch it as it passed by.

John winced. Hadn't he dug this story out of his desk – here in mild and sunny L.A., where, if he hadn't exactly distinguished himself, he'd led a life no worse than anybody else's – to lay it to rest, finally? As Annie had said, it was *old*. He'd had that insight, but as time went on it seemed less important, less useful. Once a victory, it became another kind of defeat. He had no reason for bitterness anymore. He had a wife. A son. (John hadn't wanted a son. He'd been afraid he would pass on harm to the boy. His father's curse. A girl, he'd thought, might be easier. But his fears had proved groundless.) Wasn't it time to let all the rest go?

He wished he could talk to Annie about it. During those four or five years between her divorce and his marriage, they had become as close as brother and sister could be. But Annie was dead. A secret smoker, she had died just the year before, shockingly, senselessly, in a fire in that same house on 42nd Street. A dog might have barked and awakened her, but those damned cats just ran.

They were all dead now, except for him and Tommy.

At his mother's funeral, old ladies had stood up in their pews at St. Barnabas Episcopal Church in Mount Shasta and talked of the virtues of Constance Hiller. Her kindness, her patience, her willingness to lend a hand, her embodiment of all that the Eastern Star and Delta Kappa Gamma, the teachers' sorority, stood for. John knew these women. They'd been old when he did the sump job – maybe fifty – and now they were ninety and almost unchanged. Their hair was completely white, the skin of their hands as thin and translucent as oiled paper over vein and bone. Their voices quavered. But they spoke warmly of his mother, and they meant it, he knew.

Because of all of them in the family, John thought, maybe his mother was the one who, after all, knew the secret of how to live. Quietly, steadily. You did old-lady things – you wrote thank-you notes and played bridge and went to lunches. You sent Christmas cards. You stayed in touch. And somehow, in the end, it mattered. His mother had served on the school board well into her seventies. She had sponsored two girls – one in Indonesia, one in India – through the Christian Children's Fund. She had traveled, and would talk to strangers on the street as readily in Dublin as in Dunsmuir. She had put up with his father's moods, and worried about him, John, during the war and afterward; she had managed her money, kept up the Needham Avenue house he and Tommy would inherit....

Tommy.

There was his parents' true memorial, John thought.

For as soon as Frank and Connie Hiller discovered that no special education classes were available in the South County, they lobbied hard to get some. John remembered when he and Annie first took Tommy up to the classes, in Mount Shasta. The teacher seemed surprised at the matter-of-fact way they introduced him. That surprised *them*. "Oh, you wouldn't believe," the teacher said. "We're getting kids nobody even knew existed. Kids who've been kept in closets and attics all their lives because their families were ashamed of them." Some of these children were far more afflicted than Tommy, but John and Annie were horrified nonetheless, and proud that they belonged to a different kind of family. A better one.

Then his parents helped found the Siskiyou Opportunity Center to give some of the graduates of those classes jobs. Ever since, Tommy had followed a routine. He got up at 4 a.m. and walked across the street to make coffee at the SP depot. He'd made it for his father's old friends and now made it for a second generation. Then he had breakfast and caught the "stage" to Weed, where he worked on a crew that maintained the Interstate 5 rest stop. He mowed grass, shoveled snow, cleaned toilets. Then he rode the stage back to Dunsmuir, ordered pizza or heated up a pot pie, and was in bed by 8 p.m. On weekends he walked out to his mother's house to do laundry and play DVDs. Video and cigars and steak-and-eggs breakfasts were his only indulgences. He wore sandals and shorts in almost any weather, T-shirts and quilted vests and a fluorescent orange cap. He stomped through town, swinging his arms the way his father had, gnawing a big callus on the back of his left hand and talking to himself. Tommy Hiller was a local character, liked or at least tolerated. The whole town watched out for him. His mother allowed him an illusion of independence -- an apartment of his own -- while she doled out his railroad disability money. (What Tommy thought of all this, nobody knew. He was impenetrably bluff and cheerful. Some parts of his mind seemed to be undamaged – he knew an amazing amount, for instance, about World War II aircraft.) Now John would have to take over that job.

Talking to those nice people at the funeral, he'd wondered why he still had to feel like an outsider, an exile, after all these years.

Wasn't it time to come home?

# # # #

I wasn't able to see New Orleans. Dusk came before we reached the Mississippi. We stopped less than a half-hour to change trains, change railroads, and I didn't leave the station. I'm not sure I even saw the river. I slept through Alabama and woke up in the South I always recall: *Green as home, even greener, maybe. With that weird kudzu vine, whatever it's called, growing up out of the railroad cuts and over lumps that used to be trees or telephone poles or even buildings, like camouflage netting or some kind of science-fiction crud. We must have gone through the bad side of every town, the way trains do. Red clay roads and shacks with hardly a fleck of paint left on them; just gray, weathered wood, like they hadn't gotten around to painting anything since 1865.*

I remember all this. I made a point of remembering it, so that I could tell people back home, with a little chuckle after "1865." But what about the people on the train? I try to remember them and can't. I must have been in a stupor by then. I dreamed off and on, about standing at the top of a cliff and hearing cries below. My clothes were wrinkled and sour from being slept in, and I needed a shave. It may be that I didn't talk to anyone after the couple in Texas.

[Not true. There was one more girl. One final form of embarrassment.

[She was a Negro girl, as we would have said then, in a crowd of celebrating young people who suddenly filled the car somewhere in Georgia. Their school had won a football game on the road, and they were headed home. The girl had been drinking, but she wasn't drunk. She just didn't give a damn. I talked "funny," was a California Yankee – that's what got us started. She laughed at my accent and asked what life was like on the West Coast: beach bingo parties and all. I found myself talking about Roger Grant, Dunsmuir High's star running back. He weighed only 160 pounds, but he was the Siskiyou County 100-yard dash champ, and as for *moves* – well, Gayle Sayers had nothing on Roger. We even had him run our extra points, I told the girl, smiling at what hillbillies we were; we didn't have a placekicker.

[I was trying, of course, to show her how enlightened we were outside the South, how free of prejudice I was in particular. But the more I talked, the less she seemed to like what I was saying.

["That's how white folks always are," she muttered.

["What?"

["You only think about the jocks," she said. "You only think about black people's *muscles*, how fast they can *run*, not their brains."

[I tried to deny this. It was just that Roger was special, I said.

["But you thought of him right off," she said. "You didn't think of any Negro kid who got straight A's. Any science whizzes. Now, did you?

["I d-didn't know any of those," I said.

["You see?"

[*See what?* I thought. Roger hadn't been much of a student; none of the three or four black families in town had produced a scientist, as far as I knew, but I wasn't saying they *couldn't*. I felt unfairly picked on. But at another level, I felt guilty, exposed. The more I tried to argue with the girl, the deeper the hole I was digging for myself, as deep as the sump.

[I can still see the girl standing in the aisle, one hand on her hip, the other brandishing a plastic cup of beer, rocking on the balls of her feet as the train clicked and swayed. She didn't have an Afro. She had pigtails wrapped in rubber bands, I think. A starched white blouse. Sweat shining on her forehead. She looked down at me with eyes that were calm and deadly serious. It makes me wonder. How much courage or recklessness did it take for her to talk like that to a strange white man on a train in Georgia in 1966 -- just a year after the Voting Rights Act -- even if she had other blacks there to back her up? I don't know. Maybe not as much as I think. Maybe she was a veteran protester, a Freedom Rider, even. It would have been worth finding out. I wish I'd kept on talking to her instead of pretending to be exhausted and curling up defensively in my seat.]

# # # #

We rode over the ridge in Peter Linz's truck. We reached a straight stretch a mile long, the only one on that road. The land slanted left, the sun right, in balance. I felt sleepy and peaceful, letting the throb of the steering wheel and the pressure of Karin's leg sink into me. Ahead was another pickup, so far ahead that I didn't notice it until, deliberately, it turned left. *My God*, I thought without any sense of alarm. *He's going right out into space.* Then a car materialized out of the shimmer on the road, coming the other way, too close to swerve. It hit the truck broadside, with a crisp, almost musical sound; light seemed to spray off them like water. Then they both plunged over the embankment.

A little dust rose over the top. Otherwise, nothing. I still chugged along. *If I'd been alone, I might have thought I was seeing things*, I sometimes say. *I might not have stopped.* But I would have, I know. That part was easy. Karin and Ned just made it easier. I parked on the shoulder opposite the skid marks and glass, ran across the road and looked down.

The Forest Service had bulldozed the manzanita there and planted seedling pines. The bulldozers had plowed up parallel ridges of dead brush and dirt. The pickup and the car had landed on the first ridge, both upside down. The truck was dark green, I think; the car some pale color. The people had been thrown out. Three or four of them. I'm not sure how many, because right from the beginning I was trying to blank them out. They were moving in the dust among the baby trees, not quite crawling but moving, writhing as if on fire but in slow motion, and they made sounds. *Like they were faking*, I always say. *I knew they weren't but ... they made these weird half-hearted sounds, like kids only pretending to be hurt.*

I stood there in the wind blowing across the slope and booming in my ears. The air seemed dense, as if under tons of pressure. And just as I'd always known would happen, every first-aid course I'd ever taken – at the town pool and in the Boy Scouts and just the previous summer at Fort Lewis – was squeezed out of me. I remembered nothing. I closed my eyes, and when I opened them again everything I saw seemed tinged with purple, like that cabin door at Castle Lake. The air around the two wrecks vibrated with heat or gasoline fumes. I had the strange impression that the whole scene was a photograph, curling at the edges, about to burst into flame. The people still moved; their sounds hadn't stopped.

I turned away.

Two or three other cars had arrived. Thank God.

"I'm going in for help," I yelled.

I didn't yell at the other drivers, quite, or at Karin or Ned. I sort of yelled in between them. But it came out loud and clear, without any stutter. I remember that. One of the only two times in this whole story I spoke well, and it came when I was running away.

I climbed back into the truck. Karin and Ned stared at me. I started up. Did they say anything? They must have, yet I only see their faces bouncing beside me and hear the golf clubs clinking in the bed behind. It can't be true, I think even now, but maybe it was. Maybe I'd succeeded more than I knew. Maybe that John Wayne act had really made them think I was logger-tough and stuffed full of military lore. So that now, in a crisis on my home ground, they deferred to me. To my *leadership*.

What a joke. Because they must have realized what I did before the other cars were out of sight: that we were the last people who should have gone, if time counted for anything. I pushed the truck to 55. That was all it would do. I mashed down on the throttle and shoved against the wheel in a parody of race driving, as if my own tugging and sweating could make us go faster. It was three miles to the town of Mount Shasta. I tried to look at Black Butte ahead of us, then at the tepee burner and log piles of the mill crawling by on the left – anything to ignore the faint outlines of those people still moving across my eyes. Later, as the engine groaned and bucked, I thought of Peter Linz. That grave, calm face, that thin mustache. I tried to comfort myself with the idea that a man who had already suffered so much, had his arm shot off, would forgive me if I blew up his truck.

We made it to the city hall. Cedars and stonework and a World War I cannon in front, like the one in Dunsmuir. I parked, and we all piled out and hurried in to police headquarters. I tried to tell the cop at the desk. I had the words all ready, lined up in my mind, but now, when it meant the most, my voice failed utterly. I whined and twitched, looked away, stamped my foot, turned red in the face; I was at the point of dissolving when Karin took over. She said what had to be said. At that moment her cheek was so close to mine that I could feel the warmth of it and smell the perfume and see that fine golden down. It was like some final intimacy, but when she finished and I dared to look straight at her, I saw the face of a stranger.

The cop got on the phone. I was turning to go when he said, "Wait a minute."

I stopped.

"You. Wait a minute," the cop said. "You said you live around here?"

I nodded.

"Just curious," the cop said. "But why did you come all the way in to us?"

Then I remembered.

"You went right past the CHP office. You've gotta know where that is. They've got the ambulance," the cop said. "You went right past 'em. Wasted, I don't know, five minutes, anyway. You'd better just hope it doesn't make any difference."

# # # #

I've never been back that way again, so my memory of the cities on my route hasn't changed. Washington, D.C., is misty lights in the middle of the night. Philadelphia, you may be surprised to hear, is beautiful: red smokestacks above calm water at dawn. In New York, we stopped at Penn Station for 40 minutes to change trains. It was Sunday morning. I climbed out to find the financial district almost deserted: blackened stone facades and the filthiest streets I'd ever seen, littered with newspapers. I saw a tower a way off and wondered if it was the Empire State Building. I started walking. The tower seemed to recede at the same speed. I walked faster. At its marble base, I gawked. *What a hillbilly.* It was the Empire State Building. I had just enough time to walk back to the station, and that is Manhattan.

When we arrived at South Station in Boston, it was mid-afternoon. I took a taxi. The driver grunted as he tossed my suitcases into the trunk.

"Harvard Square," I said.

That was the second thing I said well. I said it clearly and jauntily, the way a student going there should.

But that was all. That was the last of the excitement. The driver repeated, "Hahvahd Square," in that Kennedy accent that, it turned out, only townies used. He said it like a question, as if he had his doubts. And I saw his point. I huddled in my shabby clothes in the back seat as the meter clicked and we wound through streets *that follow the original cow tracks, they say.* We somehow missed seeing the fine buildings along the Charles River. When he finally stopped, it seemed to be in just another sooty tangle of city. An MTA station, cafeterias, bookstores. He grunted again as he pulled the suitcases out, and I overtipped him with almost the last of the sump money.

Then I saw that I'd misunderstood. The square was crowded with people, students and otherwise. The driver hadn't questioned my right to be there; he'd just laughed at a rube like me, riding all the way across the city when I could have taken the subway for a tenth as much.

Maybe.

I don't know. I shouldn't even try to guess. I had a map of the campus, but the taxi was gone before I realized that the dorm where I was to stay, near the law school, was still a half-mile north on Massachusetts Avenue. That winter a lawyer for an insurance company visited me there and took my deposition. Two of the people in the accident had died. The pickup's steering gear had snapped, he said. He wanted to know if the car had had time to turn. I said no. I felt fairly sure of that. He wrote it down and left. Nobody blamed me.

I can't remember being warm in Cambridge again, but that afternoon it was steaming. I dragged the suitcases along a bumpy brick sidewalk beside a brick wall, then beside a rail fence of black iron pipe. When I glanced in a gate, I saw what had to be the famous Yard, with grass as patchy as the greens at McCloud. It didn't look like much. I hiked on, past a park with statues and even older cannon than our city halls had. Civil War? [No, the Revolution. George Washington had taken command of the Continental Army on that very spot.] I hadn't had a bath in six days, and the dissolution I had felt at the Mount Shasta police station seemed to start all over again. The handles of the suitcases cut into my fingers; sweat blotched my shirt, leaked out of my armpits, stung my eyes. I stank.

Once more I was like a golem, a mud-man trailing slime on the pavement behind me. But I could no longer imagine that I was an avenger of the downtrodden, including myself. That summer when *everything seemed about to change*, nothing had. I was tired and homesick and scared. And Harvard? Harvard was supposed to be the bridge to my future, but I could see no future beyond Vietnam, where I knew I would go soon after my year here was up, and where I knew that I would do badly. Yet I also knew that, unlike so many others in my generation, I wouldn't be able to avoid the war or protest it. What my mother's last remark seemed to imply was true. I was a child. I would do as I was told. And neither my father's faith nor Tony Sirianni's dynamite was enough to get me out of the hole I was in.

# # # #

I had to do it myself. That's what I think now. And sometimes I think there was never a better chance than the day of Gabrielle's wedding. I did climb out of the sump, leave the truck at home and cross George West's bridge. Again, *time got mixed up*. Instead of twilight, now, I remember the sun slanting at the same angle as the mountain. I remember how the river seemed to smell as well as look brown-green. It was cool in the willows there. I crossed the railroad tracks and headed up a trail. I did that much.

What the clown sees just before: I saw oaks and pines and firs and the rocks of the trail, and a creek that fed into the river. I climbed higher and saw my home town already far away: the ballpark and the pool. I saw myself, walking, being pierced by bullets of light that streamed through the branches, parallel to the slope, in air clearer than I ever see today. Higher still, I saw where somebody had sighted in a .30-06, firing at beer bottles against a clay bank; I picked up a cartridge case, golden in the light, and sniffed it. A faint smell of gunpowder.

I was getting into manzanita now. I remember thinking of how it would tear at my clothes, then at my skin. Then I thought of how years ago my father and a friend [A.B. Jones, no relation to Bud] had gone deer hunting in brush like this. The friend shot a bear, and the only way they could wrestle the heavy carcass to the nearest logging road was to cut it in half. I saw the skinned halves of the bear hanging on hooks in the friend's garage: rigid and bluish, with muscles just like a human being's.

Was that it? The vision of the bear, the great shadow beginning to creep out from the mountain, the first chill of evening? Was that all? Or did I think about Harvard and Karin and my father, or simply about all the trouble and worry I would cause? I wish I knew. As hard as I try to remember, I can't. All I know is that the trail flattened out and started down; I followed it with the idea that it would turn uphill again, but it didn't. It was like a trajectory, and I was a dud shell, aimed at the Forest Service lookout on the peak of Bradley but falling far short. I don't remember having any thoughts at all.

Whenever I tell this story....

[But as I said before, I *didn't* tell it, really, except here.]

...I say: *It turns out the heart isn't as strong as the stomach. I managed to get back down across the river by dinnertime. So nobody knew about it but me.* That's what I say to anyone who will listen. With that same little chuckle. Even if there isn't anybody. Even if I'm just saying it to myself, here in my apartment in L.A. [I was still single when I wrote this, and lived in a series of dumps], after work that, for the record, isn't teaching after all -- saying it with a fluency I could never match in real life. Even then I can't tell this part of the story without a twinge of embarrassment, a protective irony. How stupid it all was!

Doo-wop songs.

But what if I'd kept going? That's what I find myself thinking more and more as time goes by. I think: What if I had? Not to die, I mean. To survive: to break through first into solitude and then into such an uproar and strangeness, so much humiliation, that I could never go back to the person I'd been. It might have been worth it....

[And yet, and yet.

[A dozen-odd years afterward, apparently, I still hadn't realized how cruel and selfish my plan had been -- how if I *had* died out in the woods, or tried to, Gabrielle's memory of her wedding would have been spoiled forever. And for what? Because I loved her? I was right, I think now, to begin to doubt this down in the sump, though my feeling for her was one of the biggest emotions of my life. It was this feeling, not Gabrielle herself, that I really loved. It gave me a seductive and treacherous freedom, a social outcast's consolation prize. If nobody wanted me, I could lay claim to anybody I damn well pleased. I hardly knew her. I was unwilling just to be her friend (though, thank God, I changed my mind eventually), and friendship – no more – was what she'd offered.

[No, it was the prompting of simple humanity, not some shameful failure to do the radical and romantic thing, that brought me back down the mountain that evening.

[Decency. Common sense. My mother's virtues.

[As for Harvard, it's true that I didn't make much use of my year there, in a career or networking sense. Vietnam did lie ahead of me, and some bad years after that. But that earlier John Hiller must have got caught up in the gloomy momentum of his story. To say that "all the excitement" ended when I told the cab driver, "Harvard Square" – well, that's just bullshit. I was thrilled to be there.

[A number of good things happened to me at Harvard. It was my first extended stay in a big city. I went to foreign movies and art museums. I was on "full ride," and for the first time in my life had some spending money. And the Jews forgave me, in the person of Miles Tepper, a pre-law student from New York who had an apartment, an open bottle of Chivas Regal and a passion for chess. We played regularly, and when I trusted him enough to confess my former ignorance, he laughed. "In Manhattan," he said, "I was almost the same age before I realized that the Jews were actually a minority in America. Everybody I knew – and I mean *everybody* – was Jewish."

[And there was a girl. An actual girlfriend.]

John met her in class; she was in the same M.A.T. program. They talked on a streetcar. She seemed to like him. He didn't know why. Suddenly all the laws that for so long had governed his life as strictly as the force of gravity were repealed. It was magic, like the Bear River Grade or those fluent two weeks at Fort Lewis, and at first he didn't believe in it. Surely it would end the first time he blinked. But it lasted several months. They talked – talked easily, talked a very great deal, talked even when they lay in each other's arms on the floor of her apartment while her pet gerbil spun frantically on the creaking wheel in its cage, above a pile of wood shavings, squeaking as if aroused by the sight of them.

They didn't sleep together. He had caught her, as people said, on the rebound. She had slept with her previous boyfriend, whom she would later get back together with and marry; so in *her* story John Hiller was just a pleasant interlude, somebody who wouldn't make too many demands on her. But this proved to be just what he needed. A full-blown affair would have scared him half to death. It was enough to learn, absurdly late, that talking and kissing could go together; that he could be friends with somebody who gave him an erotic charge he'd never felt with Gabrielle. They took long walks. They went to mixers, to ethnic cafés, to those foreign movies. She invited him to her parents' house in acres of woods near Concord. She didn't consider her family rich – just a touch above middle class – but they were the richest people he'd ever known, and this did matter, though he tried to pretend it didn't.

Once he happened to notice her eye shadow and said, "I like that green stuff on your eyes."

And the next time he met her – she was leaning against that same black-pipe fence by the Yard he'd passed, dragging his suitcases, on his first day there – she had it on her eyelids. This wasn't a chance meeting. She was expecting him. They were going to hear jazz together. So she must ... she must ... (his mind almost refused to grapple with this unprecedented fact) ... she must have applied it *on purpose.* To please *him.* And this knocked John silly with love. He didn't know it was love. He still thought love, to be real, had to be an unrequited misery. But what else could this be? She leaned back gracefully, an athlete, resting her elbows on the topmost pipe, wearing black tights, a black turtleneck, a rust-colored miniskirt. Beneath her short dark hair, her face and neck were flushed with November cold. On a campus of sallow intellectuals, she was strikingly healthy. She swam, fenced, rode horseback. She smelled of Oil of Olay and of something else, something indefinable, her own. She grinned up at him. And John Hiller could feel the sickness begin to drain out of him, sickness he hadn't known he had, oozing gently out as if from a hidden abscess. It would come back, often enough, but this was the moment when he learned it could go away, too.

Printed in the United States
67890LVS00001B/106-138